WATERS OF LIFE

Waters of Life

Shanon L. Mayer

First Printing, 2025

Cover design by JD&J Design

ISBN: 978-1-958076-27-9, 978-1-958076-28-6, 978-1-958076-29-3

Published by Shanon L. Mayer, Vancouver WA 98663

https://shanonlmayer.com

Books by Shanon L. Mayer

<u>Chronicles of the Chosen</u>
Sphere of Power
Veil of Deception
Reflections of Doubt
Palace of Stone

<u>Jen Rice</u>
Captives and Prisoners
Festival of Souls
Beautiful Monsters
Mind Games

<u>Inland Sea</u>
Star of Darkness
Eyes of Midnight
Grand Coven
Waters of Life

<u>Shadow Tribunal</u>
Diamond Queen
Worth More Dead

This book is for anyone who has ever been weighted down under impossible odds, who has known the responsibility for the life of another person, or who has ever felt the agony of knowing that your best efforts didn't automatically lead to the best outcome.

Special thanks to Aaron, who understood why the flute was important.

1

"This one is nice, I suppose."

"Yes, that is a good choice indeed. Made of the finest Gaon Ebony wood."

She ran her hand over the smooth, warm surface. For wood, carved from the trunk of a tree, it was surprisingly soft and smooth, as though it had been coated in the finest silk. The color was deep, fathomless black that seemed to absorb all of the available light, releasing none in reflection. Looking closely, she could see the grain but only faintly. "I'm not sure I like the idea of it being black. Can we look at something a little brighter, perhaps?"

"Of course." He set the black block onto a stack of other colored pieces of wood and brought out a different sample, this one much paler with an almost orange hue. "How about this one? Lacewood is a nice color, both pale and bright and it has such a lovely feminine pattern." Lighter-colored splotches covered the surface in a pleasing, rhythmic pattern, no doubt leading to its name. To her, it looked more like ripples on the water during a blustery day than it did lace of any variety, but she hadn't been asked her opinion when naming the wood.

Keyt's mind was swimming through all of the options she had been given. Who knew there were so many different types of wood? Each of them was lovely in its own right, in almost every color found in nature and then others she hadn't been previously aware of. Some were polished to a high gloss and others were matte, softer and less shiny. They were all nice, any oof them she had been shown would work just fine, but none of them seemed to be what she wanted.

What she really wanted, if she was honest with herself, was to not be there, not be making the decision.

She closed her eyes, as though trying to block the scene before her, visually rejecting the decision she knew must be made. "The lacewood looks great, let's go with that."

"Wonderful, just wonderful. And for the interior?" Yet another of his endless boxes of samples joined the stack of rejected wooden pieces on the table.

Keyt was in no mood for more samples, more decisions she didn't want to make. "White satin," she said. "It's traditional and simple." The scent in the shop, intended to be warm, inviting, and soothing was instead cloying, clouding her already-addled senses and increasing the heaviness that had already spread throughout her body. She couldn't wait to get back outside in the fresh air where she could breathe freely but she couldn't leave until this task was done.

If she left now, she wasn't sure she would come back.

"Are you certain? We have so many lovely fabrics lately, I'm positive you will find something more to your liking." Already rifling through his new box of samples, he began pulling out small squares of fabric for her to inspect.

She shook her head. "No. White satin."

"All right," the salesman relented and placed the samples back into the box. "We can have this ready for you in just a few days. Is it an..." he paused, "urgent need?" For the first time, his voice had inflection, while still low and melodious, his tone had shifted slightly at the question.

"A few days should be fine. She's not going anywhere."

As he tallied up the total due for her purchases, Keyt glanced around the showroom, her eyes moving from display to display, wondering which of the pieces in the showroom would end up hers when the time came. Most were made of materials she could identify from the stack of samples she had just been examining only moments before, but others were different, ones she hadn't looked at before making her decision. All of them showed excellent craftsmanship and were kept in pristine condition.

Or, more likely, which of them she would end up purchasing for Malec when his time came as well. She closed her eyes again, rejecting that thought as forcefully – if not more so – than the decision she had already been facing. Making one decision today was more than difficult enough, she didn't need to compound the stress by adding another difficult choice on top of it.

"Brass finishings, I presume?" Unnoticed, the salesman had pulled out another box of samples, his hand hovering just over the top of it as though he wasn't sure she wanted to see anything further. Had Keyt been in a more questioning mood, she would have wondered at how many boxes of samples the man had, or where he kept them all.

"Of course," she replied automatically. Brass finishings or bronze, she didn't care. Even the wood she had selected didn't matter, nor did the satin upon which she had been so insistent. When all was said and done, none of the decisions she had made that day would have any impact on anything. Nobody would appreciate the time she had already spent agonizing over this decision, the choices she had made, wondering whether they were correct. Nobody would appreciate the constant need to swallow her stomach back into place at the smell of the flowers, vases stuffed with blooms and greenery that were everywhere.

When the shopkeeper explained the final total for her selection, she could have choked at the number. Perhaps she should have gone with a cheaper wood after all. She paused for a moment, wondering whether or not it was too late to change her mind about her choices. In the end, however, it didn't matter. She had made her decision and she would stand by it. After all, she could afford to pay his exorbitant price. Even if she was certain he had marked up his prices substantially. There was no way wood, even imported wood, could cost that much.

She counted out the tyros, carefully arranging them into orderly stacks of ten for him to confirm. Once all of the stacks had been placed on the counter, she added a trio of silver thalers to complete the transaction.

"You will deliver this, I assume?" She looked up to meet his eyes for the first time since her arrival at the shop. She certainly hoped that would be part of the purchase price, as she wasn't sure how she would handle it otherwise. Delivery was the least of the services he could offer, considering how much she had just paid him.

"Of course. Do not worry; we will take care of everything from here." As it had been throughout the whole conversation, his voice was low and modulating, meant to be soothing, but it did little to help Keyt's mood. If anything, his voice had the opposite effect, grating on her and causing her even more stress than she had otherwise been experiencing.

Satisfied, if not pleased, she tucked the purse back into her pocket, quickly walked across the showroom floor and stepped out the door onto the busy street beyond. She took a deep breath of the clean air, thankful that it no longer smelled of pungent flowers. On the narrow walkway beyond the door, pedestrians walked past her, some in a hurry but most enjoying a lazy morning, in no rush to get from place to place. Almost none of them spared Keyt so much as a sideward glance as they passed by. A handful of carts rattled down the street, pulled by horses who were equally unhurried. Across the street, children played tag, chasing each other around and laughing. The clouds that had covered the sky, delivering the early morning rains, had drifted further away, now small and peaceful in the distance.

As with most people, Keyt was dressed in warm furs to guard against the impending winter weather. Her thick boots, with heavy soles designed for slogging through the mud, were an exception to the norm in town but not unusual enough to warrant suspicious glances. Her long hair, the same shade of dark brown as almost everyone around her, hung down her back in a thick braid. A few tendrils came loose in the light wind and she tucked them behind her ears to keep them out of her face.

Keyt turned to walk down the street toward home, her steps slow and steady as she went. There was no need to hurry, as the most important events had already taken place. Her mind was still murky, her thoughts filled with the activities of the past few days and wondering what she should do next. This had been her last stop, the task she had dreaded the most, and now her business was complete. There was nothing left for her to do, no further arrangements to be made, until the ceremony. She felt drained, as though she had spent the entirety of her life force over the last few days. As prepared as she had believed herself to be, making all of the arrangements had been far more exhausting than she had expected.

The air held a thin tang, the annual promise of snow was still far off in the distance but headed closer every day. Soon, the streets and buildings would be covered in a heavy white winter blanket. The foxes and other summer creatures in the nearby forest would disappear, replaced by winter wolves and snow rabbits, animals more suited to the cold. She would have to go out into the woods soon as well, the traps needed to be checked and replaced before the snow arrived.

The sight of smoke, lazily drifting toward the clouds, welcomed her home. The house her family lived in, as with most houses in the area, was long and low, a single room that stretched from one end of the building to the next. From inside, she barely had to stretch in order to reach the beams that formed the roof overhead, which made simple work of the regular patching that it required. Fireplaces made of stone and brick were set into either end of the house, both of which had been lit so to make the interior cozily warm and welcoming. Much as she wanted to go inside, the reindeer needed to be tended, so she walked around the house and to the open area beyond, heavy boots crunching through the light coating of frost that had settled over the valley following the morning shower.

"Hey, big fella." She reached out a hand toward the first big buck she encountered. This particular buck had been with her family for years and had sired many of the foals bouncing through the meadow. She walked through the herd, careful to not scare any of them and start a stampede. Although it had been years since she had made that mistake, the lesson had been well-learned and she hadn't needed a repeat lesson.

A couple of the foals were doing better than she had expected, each of them standing strong and tall already. These had been born late in the season and she had been worried about whether they would be strong enough to survive the winter, so seeing them up and agile already was heartening. One was still unsteady on its feet and she moved closer to examine it, concerned about both its health and its safety. "If you don't get a bit stronger soon," she explained, "the wolves will be able to catch you."

Of course, she knew the reindeer couldn't understand her. She wasn't capable of communicating directly with them, but she still felt as though they could understand what she meant. Something about their big brown eyes and the way they watched her as she went about her business held a sense of knowing, as though they comprehended far more than most realized. Whether it was true or not, she still spoke to them, letting them know what she was doing whenever she approached their pen or had to go inside for any purpose, whether that was a wellness check on the foals or breaking the ice on their water trough. It was also because of that reason that she was particularly careful with her words whenever she brought one of the creatures to the slaughterhouse. The less the herd knew of what was happening, the better off they all were.

Once she finished examining the reindeer foals, satisfied that they were healthy and would continue to grow in both size and energy, she turned to head into the house. There were no windows to allow light in from outside, as all of the doorways were covered with heavy skins in anticipation of the colder weather that had finally arrived. Malec waited inside, sitting in his favorite chair next to one of the fires and shuffling the embers with a poker. A black kettle was suspended by a hook so that it hung just barely over the embers, high enough to not be touched by the flames when another log was added but low enough for the embers to keep its contents warm.

Malec was older than Keyt by one year, but he had a weak constitution and didn't leave home very often. While she tended to any business that needed to be done in town, he remained behind to care for the livestock, maintain the household and prepare the meals. Since he was inside, he wore only the lighter underlayers of clothing but he had a thick woolen blanket on his lap to keep the chill from his bones. Unlike the wide frame of most men of the northern lands, Malec was thin and appeared every bit as frail as he truly was.

"How did it go?" he asked when he saw her.

"About as well as it could have, I suppose."

He nodded quietly and watched as she picked up a bowl from the counter and ladled some soup from the kettle. "Any problems?"

"No," she shook her head. "Everything's arranged, so now all we need to do is wait for the ceremony." Her bowl sufficiently filled, she carried it with her as she went back to the counter to fetch a spoon.

"When is it scheduled for?"

"Four days from now. Everything will be delivered to the site and laborers will start on setting up the temporary framework tomorrow." She settled at the low table and sniffed, inhaling the rich scent. Late season squash, potatoes and golden beets, one of her personal favorites. It even smelled as though it had a bit of peppercorn for spice as well. "This smells delicious."

He joined her at the table, matching bowl in hand, and they ate in silence. Occasionally the meal was interrupted by snippets of conversation, but those were few and far between. Long gone were the days of raucous conversation and arguments over the last heel of bread, the siblings were no longer children and no longer needed to act as such.

"I don't think I want to go," Malec said finally.

"You have to go," Keyt responded without hesitation. "It's mother. You can't just ignore this."

"I know." Frustration dripped from his voice. "It's not that I want to ignore this, I just don't know if I can handle it."

"You can." She reached a reassuring hand out to cover his. "You can and you will. I will be there to support you; I'll always be there for you. You know that."

"I just…" his voice broke. "I feel so lost right now."

"Me too. But I think that's normal." She passed him another piece of bread, along with a pat of freshly-churned butter. "And it's going to feel this way for a while but eventually things will return to normal."

Rather than responding, he picked up his bowl and hers, along with both spoons, and carried them over to the wash-bucket. "The worst part," he said once the dishes were clean, "is that, for us, this is normal. Completely, perfectly normal." All traces of anger were gone, instead he just sounded tired. More than tired, really. He sounded as though he was thoroughly exhausted just by the idea.

She couldn't argue with him. His words were true. Although she hadn't said as much, everything he had expressed were feelings she herself had been experiencing. Unlike her brother, she hadn't said anything about her mental state, as there was simply no point. Nothing either of them could do would change what had happened, nor could they change what was to come.

2

The sun rose, sending waves of pink and orange shimmering across the cold blue sky. A few clouds made an appearance overhead, fewer still were the people gathered at the base of the low hill. Keyt was there, as was Malec, despite his previous argument. He had spent almost a full day abed in preparation for this morning. Not that there had been much to warrant his attention in the meantime. All of the details had already been attended to.

A handful of others arrived, including Raggan, the local cleric. His face and hair were covered with the ceremonial cowl and he carried his prayer beads and an assortment of other items Keyt didn't recognize. He entered the area wafting smoke around him as he traveled, fumes from the burning herbs in the censor he carried quickly dispersing in the open area. Behind the cleric came four men carrying a large lacewood box by its brass handles. Although the box was closed and sealed, Keyt knew precisely what was inside. She had selected everything personally from the wood to the satin sheets to the clothing her mother wore to the handful of precious trinkets placed with her. Nothing had been overlooked, every detail tended to.

The bearers placed the box onto the ground, settling the pale wooden box next to a deep rectangular opening in the soil. The ground was already cold enough that the diggers had been concerned, uncertain that they would be able to complete the excavation before the frost fully hit and encased the valley in ice, but to everyone's relief they had prevailed and been successful. None of the other townspeople came to mourn or say farewell and even the bearers, once the coffin had been delivered, made a hasty retreat.

Once the hill was silent, Raggan said a brief prayer, his rough voice encouraging the soul of the deceased to move along to the hereafter in peace. As he spoke, he scattered an assortment of

herbs and other items across the top of the casket, the same herbs that continued to burn into
incense next to him as he spoke. The litany was
common, as all knew, but this time there was
more behind the words. The townspeople were
afraid, and they had every right to be. Had she
been in their position, Keyt would probably be
afraid as well.

Death wasn't frightening, as everyone understood that life was fleeting and that people died
on occasion. It was simply a conclusion, the necessary passage from one life into the next. What
the townspeople feared was not the act of death
itself but instead the affliction that had taken the
woman in the casket at such a young age. Their
fears were of the disease that had come to be
called the Wasting for the way it gnawed away at
a person until their body gave up entirely. While
alive, those inflicted with the Wasting were safe
to have in their midst as the disease wasn't trans-
ferrable easily from person to person. Once dead,
however, the body's natural breaking-down
process released the disease into the nearby area
and those who encountered it could become ill.

That chance of infection was the only reason that necessitated a coffin. Coffins could be sealed tightly and placed safely underground, far out of reach from everyone. That was why the small group gathered in the valley rather than celebrating the life that had passed on the next hilltop over where the more common sky burials were done. Here, the dead woman was treated as unclean, despite all of the good she had done for the townspeople over the course of her life. Because she had fallen to the Wasting, she no longer belonged among them.

Once Raggan finished his speech and prayer, Keyt pulled out her wooden flute. The flute was the greatest gift her mother had given her, an instrument that had been carved by one of her ancestors and passed down from mother to daughter for generation upon generation. Her fingers ran over the intricate carvings that spiraled around the length of the instrument, carvings that had become as familiar to her as the lines that crisscrossed her own palms. She had no idea how many breaths had been used to bring forth music from the flute from her mother and her mother's mother before her, but her own joined them in perfect symphony. She played the song of mourning, letting the music inscribe in the air all of the pain she felt inside, pain she couldn't adequately share with words alone. She played as tears streamed down her cheeks and dripped to the toes of her boots on the frost-covered ground below. She played in the hopes that her mother could hear her song one last time and be encouraged to find a better life beyond this one of sickness and sadness, of fear and distrust, of loneliness and silence. She played until her air was gone and she could play no longer.

As the coffin slipped into its final resting place and the first spadefuls of frozen earth was cast in to cover it, she turned away. She didn't want to think of her mother that way, locked beneath the ground and hidden away like a most privately guarded secret for an eternity.

"We're headed for the tavern." Malec wrapped an arm around her in an attempt to bring comfort, but Keyt wasn't interested in comfort. She shook him away and stepped apart from the group.

"I need to go water the reindeer," she explained. "The watering hole is frozen over."

"I'll go with you."

"No," she shook her head, not bothering to wipe away the residual traces of moisture on her cheeks. "You go on ahead to the tavern. I'll catch up with you once I'm done."

Despite her argument, he accompanied her back to the house and they quickly broke open the ice-covered watering holes, much to the relief of the herd. The big males came first, followed as usual by the small foals. To Keyt's relief, the smallest of the foals had steadied on his feet and trotted along behind, nosing his way through the herd to get his own place at the hole. She had been worried that he would hang back behind the herd, unable to push his way to the water.

"There is something else," Malec pointed out as he leaned on one of the fence rails. "It's about Leoni." Rather than looking at his sister, he gazed into the distance, letting his eyes roam over the herd of reindeer. The first flakes of snow began to fall and he watched them descend in silence.

Keyt looked up at him in surprise. "What happened to Leoni?" Although the woman hadn't been at the burial ceremony, she had assumed it was due to the possibility of infection. She didn't hold it against the woman; had she made an appearance, Keyt likely would have suggested she leave with the bearers to minimize any sort of contamination. Much as she didn't enjoy the distance at which the townspeople kept themselves from her family, she understood their motivations. She would rather not have others there than risk infection by their presence.

"She wishes to marry."

Keyt blinked a few times, trying to understand the problem. "Of course she wishes to marry. Why is that a problem?" She jerked around with a start. "Wait a moment, are you saying she wishes to marry someone else?"

"No, of course not."

"Oh." She should have known better. Leoni and Malec had been in love since they had first met as children. Had either of them ever so much as looked at another in a romantic sense, Keyt would have been amazed. "So, what is the problem?"

"She also wants to start a family."

"That's a wonderful idea. You will make a terrific father. And husband, of course."

"I told her I wouldn't do it." Despite Keyt's scrutinizing gaze, he refused to meet her eyes, continuing to focus on the other end of the pasture and the flecks of white that continued to fall. It wasn't enough snow to cause either of them worry, so his continued attention on the snowfall was intended only to keep him from looking directly at his sister.

"Why would you tell her that?" She was appalled. Never had she expected for Malec and Leoni to not be wed one day. "She is a great match for you."

"I know. And I adore her dearly. But that is precisely why I can't do this to her."

"Do what?"

"Will you have me leave her a widow?" he demanded, finally turning his eyes toward his sister. "Or my children fatherless?" He swallowed hard before continuing. "What if one of them is born with the Wasting? What would you have me do then?"

"Calm down," she took a step closer to him. She had never heard that level of despair in his voice before and it unnerved her to hear it now. "I understand your concerns."

He blinked rapidly, trying in vain to hold the shine in his eyes from turning into the threatening torrent of tears. "I don't know what to do. If I don't marry her, she will find someone else. Any man would be lucky to have her. But if I do… I can't think but to worry for what might happen." His voice was every bit as thick with emotion as the tears causing his eyes to glisten.

"You and I both know that any children you have will not inherit the Wasting. You are worried for nothing. They will remain safe and healthy, as will she."

"But what if something changes? What if we are wrong and I do give it to them?"

"What if the ground falls out from beneath our feet? What if the sun refuses to rise in the morn? What if the reindeer sprout wings and fly away?" She swept her arm toward the herd as she spoke, causing the big male to look up at her in curiosity. She hoped she hadn't just given the buck any ideas.

"What?" He finally looked at her, confusion outweighing everything else on his mind. Hopefully it had also shaken him out of the spiral he'd been on the verge of.

"You're rambling on about what to do if something really, really unlikely happens. I'm just trying to help you come up with some more scenarios, each equally as likely to happen as those you are so concerned about."

He blinked at her for a long moment before sighing. "You're right," he admitted. His shoulders, held back in stubborn steadfastness during the conversation, slumped in defeat.

"Of course I'm right," she smiled weakly at him, the best she could muster for the first smile she had given anyone in the last four months. "You and I both know full well that this affliction is passed down from the mother only. Leoni doesn't have it and isn't likely to catch it, so your children won't get it. Not now, not ever."

"Is that why you don't socialize with the men in town?"

She nodded. "I will not marry; I will have no children. This Wasting ends with me. I refuse to force a single person to experience what you and I have already experienced." She turned back to finish watering the reindeer, sliding one hand down the soft fur of the smallest foal. "The family curse ends with me."

3

After they finished tending to the reindeer and the conversation that accompanied the tending, Keyt and Malec went to the tavern, just as he had originally intended to do. She needed a drink quite badly and he was eager to see his lady. As she watched the two of them disappear into a quiet corner, Keyt's mind was filled with the future the two of them would share, one filled with happiness and, she hoped, lots of children. Her brother deserved no less.

She listened in on snippets of conversation from the men gathered there. It was still early enough that the raucous crowd hadn't yet arrived, so most of the patrons were simply travelers who stopped for a meal along their journey or traders recently in town for business. It was also too early in the day for music, so the tavern was blessedly quiet. As she settled into a rough wooden chair at a table near the back of the tavern, her stomach reminded her that she had skipped breakfast that morning, due in no small part to the stress of the burial ceremony, so she signaled for a plate of food to be brought along with the ale.

"I'm tellin' ya," one of the patrons at a nearby table explained to his companions. "I heard it with me own ears." The man, along with his companions, was from the northern lands, that much was obvious. Not only were they all roughly the same height and build as others in town, but they also wore the same fur and leather clothing as those used to cold wintery weather. The furs themselves weren't the same as the locals wore, but that didn't matter. While the locals primarily wore wolf and fox, these men appeared to be wearing bear.

"Sure," another responded with a hearty chuckle. "And just why would the empress drop the bounty on 'im?"

"Maybe she's afeared," another suggested. "As I heard it, she's a little slip of a thing, probably afraid he'll come after 'er next!"

"She's got no reason to be afeared," the first disputed. "She's got one of our own up there wit' her, keepin' guard."

"One 'a ours? Who's she got?"

"Name o' Vox, from what I heard."

"Wasn't he the one who went out traveling?"

"Yep, same one. From what I heard, he met up with her out in the Inland Empire."

"Still don't make no sense. Even with one of ours with her, why would she drop the bounty? I mean, the man killed 'er own father, dinn't he?"

"Maybe," the man took a deep swig of his beer and wiped his mouth with the back of his sleeve. "But maybe not. Story tells he weren't the one who did 'im."

"You're trying to tell me," the second man leaned forward, arms crossed on top of the table, to put his face directly in front of the first man's, "that 'er father was assassinated, jus' not by an assassin?"

"Din't say he weren't killed by an assassin, jus' said maybe he weren't killed by 'im, that's all."

Already losing interest in the conversation, particularly since she had no clue who the men were discussing, Keyt turned her attention to another table. This one appeared to be men from one of the trade ships docked out in the pier, if their clothing was any indication. Instead of the heavy furs and thick leather preferred by those who lived in the cold north, these men were dressed in cotton trousers with heavy woolen cloaks clasped tightly around their shoulders for warmth. While their clothes would suffice with the current chill in the air and the meager snow that continued to fall, should the men stay too long they would discover for themselves why the locals all wore fur.

"Maybe we should head for that spring he told us about."

"I think we're a bit too late for that, I'm afraid. That spring was only supposed to help the dying, not the already dead."

"But it could help if someone else gets attacked. I mean, that loremaster said it cured all ails, so why wouldn't it work on injuries, too?"

"It's probably just a legend anyway. No point in wasting our time chasing wives' tales. We have more important things to chase."

Her interest piqued by the reference to curing ails, Keyt continued listening in on their conversation, hoping to hear more about this spring they had mentioned but there was no further discussion about it. Disappointed, she returned to her own meal. Even if the spring they had mentioned was a real thing, they hadn't said enough for her to even know what kind of power it may have. No point in wasting her time on things that didn't matter, after all. At the other end of the tavern, she spotted Leoni and Malec, still deep in conversation. It didn't appear to be going well, if the girl's tears were any indication.

"It's just not worth the risk." Malec said, his voice loud enough to reach his sister's ears. "I will not have you left alone."

Leoni tried to argue but Malec rose to his feet and strode out of the tavern. Keyt watched the interchange and his exit in surprise. When they had spoken at the reindeer pens, it sounded as though Malec would agree to the proposed marriage but what he had just said made it appear otherwise. What had caused him to change his mind yet again?

She didn't have to wonder too much about that to come up with an answer. Malec had never been particularly healthy but had remained alive in no small part due to their mother's constant attendance at his side. With her death, there was little to halt the disease that would eventually claim his life.

Why did her family have to suffer so? What god had they offended and what had they done, to deserve such a curse? If such offense had indeed been caused by someone in their lineage, had enough amends since that time not yet been made? Was there nothing that could be done to bring this nightmare to an end?

Leoni left soon after, whether to follow Malec or to return to her own home, Keyt had no idea. She stayed at her table, working her way through a mug of ale that had lost all flavor and absently chewing on a hunk of gravy-soaked bread. The meal had tasted well when it had arrived, as had the ale, but both had lost their flavor. Without needing to be told, she knew her brother was not long left for this world. She had always known he would pass shortly after their mother, but until now she hadn't spent much time considering what that loss would mean to her. Malec meant the world to her, the only family she had left now that their mother was gone.

For the first time, realization struck that she was about to be left utterly alone.

And there was nothing she could do to stop it.

Well, maybe. She paused, mug of ale halfway between table and mouth. Perhaps there was a glimmer of hope after all. If the gods had determined that enough amends had been made after all, they may have just granted an opening, the opening she had been searching for. She flicked her eyes over to a nearby table. All she needed to do now was to take it.

When the sailors stood to leave, she stood as well. She hurriedly dropped a few copper thalers onto the table, more than enough to pay for her unfinished meal, and followed them into the frigid air outside.

"Excuse me," she called after them. "May I have a word?"

She had no idea what she was doing it, or why she was doing it. These men were strangers to her, people she had not seen before that day. Not that it was a surprise to have foreigners in town, they arrived with some regularity aboard trading ships. But these men, they were different somehow, in some unfathomable way she couldn't quite identify. She just knew that these men knew something she hadn't known, something that may give her the ray of hope she had been lacking for so long. The gods had heard her heart's wish and, hopefully, they had answered it.

"What's that?" One of the sailors turned back to face her. "Can I help you?"

"I certainly hope so. I couldn't help but overhear a portion of the conversation you were having and I would like to ask a couple questions, if I may." She stopped a respectful distance away from the group, not wanting to alarm them.

"Listening in, hmm?" One of them frowned at her. He was more heavyset than his companions, likely due to the quantity of ale he had just consumed. If that was his normal habit, he was soon to need a larger belt. "We don't take kindly to eavesdroppers."

"Now calm down," another man put a restraining hand on his arm. "We weren't exactly discussing secrets or anything, now were we? And in a crowded place like that, people are bound to hear what we're talking about." He turned his attention to Keyt. "What can we help you with?" Unlike his portly friend, this man was tall and lean, well-groomed, clean-shaven and in clean clothing. He didn't even smell like the sailors he had been among, evidence of a recent bath.

"That spring you mentioned," she stepped forward eagerly, "the one with healing powers. Can you tell me more about it?"

"The spring?" The man's brows rose at her inquiry. "I'm willing to share what I know, but I'm afraid it's not very much."

"Anything you have," she answered. "I'll appreciate anything, anything at all."

As though sensing her desperation, or probably more likely recognizing that anyone so intent on discovering information about a magical healing spring was already in a desperate situation, the sailor turned to his men. "I'll meet you back on the ship soon. You guys go on ahead without me."

The men exchanged nods and shrugs before turning as a group and continuing down the road toward the docks. Once they were a few paces away, the sailor who remained behind turned back to address her once more. He pushed a lock of his blond hair, an oddity in the northern lands, to the side of his face and beamed at her charmingly. "How about you start by telling me who you are. Introductions are always the best way to begin a conversation, after all."

"Yes, of course. My name is Keyt, I live here. My brother and I were both raised here. And you are?"

"My name is Dane, Dane McClannahan. It is my absolute pleasure to make your acquaintance." If anything, his smile became even brighter.

"What can you tell me about the spring?" She wanted to be patient, to not pressure the man. After all, he had been kind enough to stay behind to speak with her. However, her patience for niceties was limited at best.

Dane McClannahan chuckled. "Right to the point, I like that. Anyway, as you may have already overheard, we don't know a whole lot about the spring. I heard stories about it when I was younger by the loremaster on my uncle's ship, back when I was working in the Inland Empire."

A tingle of excitement ran up her spine. "This loremaster, do you know his name?"

"Sure, I do. Name's Wyrm. He had loads of stories about pretty much everything you can imagine from his travels all over the empires. But I'm sad to say that the story you want to know about is one of the few that he never went into much detail on."

Keyt sighed in frustration, her brows lowering in disappointment. "So you don't really know very much about it at all, then, do you?"

"I'm afraid not, but I'm willing to share what little I do know with you."

"That would be wonderful, thank you."

"From what I understand, he came across the spring once, many years ago. Never even said which empire he was in when he found it, if I'm remembering correctly. But the local legends said that it could cure any ailment, natural or magical."

"What about curses? If an ailment was caused by a curse, could that spring heal it?"

"A curse?" He rubbed his chin thoughtfully. "Well, I can't say I really know. But if I had to guess, I'd say yes. After all, a curse is just a magical ailment, isn't it?"

It was worth a shot, she decided. Even if it turned out to be nothing, that would be better than sitting at home and waiting for Malec to die, better than buying a coffin matching their mother's for him to spend an eternity confined within, better than making burial ceremony arrangements so that he could be hidden in the ground alongside the rest of their cursed family. If there was even the slightest chance that this loremaster could have found the cure, she needed to go find it. "This loremaster, you said his name was Wyrm?"

"Correct. He spent quite a few years working with me on a ship called the Temptress while I was there."

"Where can I find him now? You said he was in the Inland Empire. Is he still on this boat of your uncle's?"

"Probably. He's older than dirt but I don't think he'll stop traveling until the gods force him to. The Temptress is based from Hoem, a little town on the Inland Sea. They usually go up and down the Pirate Run about once every other month or so."

Keyt had very little knowledge of the empires beyond Barberry, as such she had never heard of either Hoem or the Pirate Run but it didn't matter. "Is that where you are based out of as well?" When Dane nodded, she stepped closer. "Can you take me with you? Back to meet this man? I have gold, I can pay you as many tyros as you need for passage." Much as she didn't like traveling by boat, she was willing to make an exception in this case.

Dane's smile faded as he shook his head. "We only just started our run, so we won't be heading back that way for a number of months yet. Besides, tracking Wyrm down is nigh on impossible. When he's on the Temptress, he's not all that sociable and when they're in port, he's off doing his own thing. So even if I took you to him, I doubt you'd get much of anything at all."

Crestfallen, she stepped back once more. She hadn't considered that the ship they were on had been headed away from their home port rather than toward it, nor had she considered that the loremaster would be busy elsewhere while she wanted to question him. "Thank you for the information," she said, trying to keep the tone of disappointment from her voice. "You mentioned this loremaster traveled extensively, correct? Was that just within the Inland Empire, or did he travel into Barberry or Dracott as well?"

"Oh, he traveled everywhere. I know personally that he's well-versed in Barberry, but he has mentioned multiple times that he's spent a lot of time in Dracott and even Sapphire." He laughed. "If there's an empire anywhere near here, it's a pretty safe bet that Wyrm's been there."

4

Keyt spent two days at the local temple, looking through all of their records and searching for any mention of the magical spring Dane McClannahan had told her about. She found records of births, records of deaths, records of marriages and the endings thereof, and far more records of healings performed on the townspeople than she would have expected. For as hale and healthy as the northmen appeared to be, they seemed to fall under the standard array of ailments and injuries. She slowed when she came across a stack of records labeled Juleth, the name of her own mother, who had been a regular visitor to the temple for healing and rejuvenation until the Wasting had progressed too far for the treatments to continue. Those treatments had extended her life far longer than most had expected, which was still far too short in Keyt's opinion.

She stopped on the last of those entries, remembering the day well. It had seemed like any other, her mother whistling a tune as she walked back into the family longhouse to begin preparations for the evening meal. She had looked well that day, healthier than Keyt had seen her in a long time. Her eyes had been bright and her skin was clear and without the sheen of sweat that had so often been present. She had appeared healthy enough, in fact, that Keyt had initially believed her mother had been relieved of the Wasting altogether.

That initial belief hadn't lasted. Only days later, the Wasting had progressed to the point where Juleth was abed, unable to even go outside to visit with her beloved reindeer. She had remained strong, undaunted in the face of what she had known was to come.

"You must be strong," she had told Keyt. "Your brother will depend on you now."

"I will be," she had reassured the frail woman. "I will do whatever I can to ensure he gets to enjoy however much life he has been allotted."

"I know you will," Juleth had chuckled. "You've always been very reliable." A coughing fit halted the conversation briefly as Keyt fetched a fresh set of wiping cloths for her. "I worry for you as well."

"I will be fine, mother. You just get your rest and do not worry about anything. I will ensure all is cared for."

"Take this," she stretched a pale white hand from under the covers, a hand that held her precious wooden flute. "It was passed down to me, but I cannot play any longer. Take it and play it whenever you can." For years as she grew from a small child, Keyt had sat at her mother's feet, listening as she played tune after tune, wondering at the clear, beautiful music that a simple carved reed could produce. She had always known that one day she would inherit the flute, she just hadn't wanted that day to come so quickly or so suddenly.

Keyt didn't want to accept the instrument. For her to be offering it up now was an undeniable indication of how little time Juleth had left. By taking it from her mother, it felt as though she was resigning her to her death while she continued to live. But Juleth had insisted and Keyt could hardly refuse the request. That day had been the first time that Keyt had played the flute for her mother, the notes coming forth as easily and as serenely as though it was the flute itself making the sound and not the breath coming from Keyt. She played every day from that point on, ensuring that her mother was able to enjoy the sound until the day she took her final breath.

"Are you looking for something in particular?" Raggan, the same cleric who had performed the burial rites for Juleth and countless others before her, interrupted her reverie, reminding her of where and when she was. His cowl was nowhere to be seen and the cloying scent of the herbs he had used during the burial ceremony had long since faded. Now, he appeared every bit as normal as he had every other time Keyt had seen him.

"I'm not sure," she admitted. "It's probably nothing more than a rumor, but I was recently told of a magical spring, one whose water could cure any manner of ailment."

The cleric nodded sagely. As with all clerics of the temple, he was dressed in simple brown robes with a rope belt about his waist. A medallion hung over his chest, the crest of his deity shining brightly, either due to the light shining from the windows or due to the presence of his deity, Keyt couldn't tell. "I know of the spring you seek."

That was possibly the last thing she had expected him to say. She turned her attention fully toward him. "Where is it?"

"That, I am afraid, is knowledge I do not have."

"But you said..." she turned back to the table holding the records, defeated yet again. "No, I suppose you didn't say." There was a vast difference between knowing of a thing and knowing where it was. She knew of the Inland Empire but that didn't mean she knew where it was. Now that it had sailed out of harbor, she knew of the ship called the Bullfrog that Dane McClannahan and his crew had been on but not their current location. She knew of their home port called Hoem and the river called the Pirate Run, but not where either of those things could be found.

"Your mother sought that spring as well." He sighed and settled into the chair next to her. "I assume the search is related in some manner to Malec?"

Keyt nodded. "He wants to marry Leoni, and she him as well. But he fears passing the Wasting on to their children and leaving her widowed."

"I can understand that concern, at least as far as widowing Leoni. But you both have to understand that there is no possibility of him passing the Wasting on to his children." His voice was low and soft, far gentler than it had been during the burial. Keyt wondered whether everything would be tainted by that memory, colored by and compared to that day.

"I know. And he does as well. But knowledge doesn't always cause fear to distance itself."

"As I well know." He reached out and patted her hand. "I also know that the answers you seek will not be found in any of these records. Your mother searched here first."

"I should have expected as much." She considered the area nearby, wondering whether any of the other towns may contain records of the spring.

As though reading her thoughts, Raggan added, "She checked many of the temples near here as well. In fact, she probably went through all of them in the Barberry Empire."

"All of them?" Her eyes widened. How much time would that have taken, she wondered. While Barberry was less inhabited than its neighboring empires, there were still many towns that would need to be explored.

"Well, perhaps not all of them. But the vast majority, to be certain."

"Do you know how far her search went?" If Keyt really intended to go on the search for the mysterious spring, there was no need to retrace her mother's footsteps. Had Juleth uncovered a cure, or the information on where to find the magical spring, she would have used it to save herself. At the very least, had she been unable to acquire it on her own, she would certainly have told her children of its existence and how to find it themselves. For her to have done none of those things could only mean that the spring had eluded her, keeping itself hidden during her search.

"I believe she went east to Hodgeman in the Inland Empire before returning. After that, she went west as far as Dian."

Keyt nodded slowly. For her mother to have explored into the Inland Empire before turning back, there must not have been anything worth going further. That was a bit surprising, as the loremaster Dane had told her about was from the Inland Empire, but the man had also said that he traveled extensively throughout the empires, so that meant little at the end of the day. Dian was on the border between the Barberry and Dracott Empires, so that sounded like as good of a place to start as any. She stood and began returning the records to their storage places.

"I will finish cleaning up here," the cleric said. "It appears to me that you have some preparations to make."

"Thank you," she said. "I'll not soon forget this." Raggan was one of the few people in town who hadn't feared her family, as his understanding of the Wasting assured him of his safety. It would be hard to leave him behind, to travel far from her home on her own and into lands filled with the unknown. But she had to try. If her mother had made the attempt, then Keyt could do no less.

She spent the remainder of the day packing what supplies she believed she would need for the journey. Since winter was about to arrive, she packed one of the light but warm woolen blankets, not wishing to cart around heavy furs. She included a paper-wrapped package of cured and dried reindeer meat, part of a block of cheese, and a few handfuls of dried berries. While she wasn't certain how long the travel from home to Dian would take, she wasn't overly concerned about running out of food along the way. She, as with all children born to the Barberry Empire, had been taught from a young age how to hunt and trap small game, how to forage even in deep snow, and how to determine whether a plant or its berries could be safely consumed. Food was never in short supply and the snow-covered land had to be truly barren in order to not provide some form of sustenance.

"I will be gone for some time," she explained when Malec asked what she was doing. "I need to go on a journey but I will return as soon as I am able."

"Where are you going?" He sat in his usual seat, legs covered in a faded blanket that smelled faintly of reindeer. That particular blanket was his favorite and had long since worn thin from use. She would need to find him a new blanket before the next winter, she was sure. Perhaps she would find a nice one for him while she was away.

"The Dracott Empire," she replied. "At least, to start. I don't know where I will go from there. I will send word to you as I am able."

"But why now? Mother has hardly been gone a week."

"It is because of that," she smiled faintly at her brother. "Speak with Leoni. She can help care for you while I am gone."

"I will come with you." He moved the blanket aside as though preparing to stand.

"No, you won't." She gently pushed him back down to his seat. "You aren't strong enough to make this trip."

Seeing that she had her mind set, Malec ceased arguing. He watched in silence as she loaded the bag with supplies and headed out to the reindeer pen. She threw the bag onto the back of one of the strong bucks, one she knew was more than capable of carrying both her and her belongings. She tucked a quiver of arrows beneath the bag and secured it, along with her bow. "Speak with Leoni," she repeated. "You shouldn't be alone and I can't stay."

She wanted to tell him why she was leaving, the question screamed from his eyes, but she couldn't say anything more. If she failed, she wanted him to have no false hopes from her. She had never lied to her brother and while this wasn't a lie, it felt as such. "Marry her. Start a family. Do not wait for my return. Be happy while I am gone."

Finally, his true question bubbled to the surface. "Will you return?"

She led the reindeer out of the pen and toward the street that led out of town. "I will. I promise you now, I will return. You will see me again."

Malec believed her and trusted in her words, faith that was written across his face as clear and bright as the noonday sky. She only wished she had as much faith in her promise as he did. She had no way of knowing what she would face on her journey or whether she would find what she sought while he was still alive.

She could only hope that the promise she made wouldn't be the first lie she told him.

5

Only a quarter of her travel rations had been consumed by the time Keyt reached the border between the Barberry and Dracott Empires. Hunting had been sparse along the trip and she hadn't wanted to spend more time than necessary until she absolutely had to. Instead, she had stopped in many of the towns and villages along the way to gain a fresh meal and a warm bed. Used to traveling long distances by reindeer, although none previously had been as long as the journey she had just begun, she was sore and tired by the time she reached Dian. All of her muscles ached and all she wanted was a hot bath, a soft bed, and to sleep for about a week. Only two of the three options were available, so she settled for an overnight sleep instead.

Almost every other town she had stopped at, she had passed through and continued her trip after only a short rest and the occasional visit to the general store to resupply her essentials. Here in Dian, however, was the last place her mother had traveled to in her own search. There was a moment of weight, a heaviness that settled deep within her soul as she surveyed the town. This was the place in which her mother's search had ended and now it was where her own would truly begin.

Vineyards filled the hills beyond the town, visible from where Keyt stood. A series of small waterwheels moved water through a series of canals and small creeks to both the vineyards and the town itself. Despite the prosperity indicated by the presence of such expansive vineyards, the town itself didn't look any wealthier than most of the others she had been to. The exception to this was one small section of town on the edge nearest the fields, which boasted much larger houses with decorative trees placed invitingly around them. "Must be where the vineyard owners live," she quietly explained to her reindeer. "Looks like they're not too interested in sharing their bounty with the rest of their people."

After just a bit of looking, she found a relatively inexpensive inn, one that was clean enough to be free of most rodents and other pests but not so nice as to drain her purse overmuch. She had plenty of tyros to spend, her mother had seen to that, but she didn't want to spend any more coins than she had to. "At least," she thought, "not quite so soon." Expenses would occur, of that she was certain, and she needed to be frugal until they arose.

The room she was given had a small window overlooking the street in front of the building. As she looked out at the setting sun, she wondered whether it was the same establishment her mother had chosen upon her own arrival in Dian, all those years before. Until her visit to the temple and the resulting conversation with the cleric, she had never been told about her mother's travels, so she had no way of confirming her curiosity. All she could do was to imagine that she was making the same choices today.

"It's just an inn," she mentally chided herself. "Stop being so maudlin."

Another difference from what she was used to, reindeer were less common this far west. Although back home, reindeer had been the one of the primary forms of livestock and stabled mounts, there were far more horses here than there were other animals. Reindeer were much more acclimated to the colder lands northward and east but, for now, the one she had would suffice. She would ignore the stares from the people around her. After all, she was used to being an object of curiosity. Now they were simply curious for different reasons.

She considered checking in the town to see if it held any of the information she sought, but then decided against it. Her mother had already been here, so any information would have already been brought home with her. There was neither reason nor time to waste here for more than just a simple night of rest.

After a night on a soft bed, at least softer than the rocky ground outside, and a refreshing breakfast of porridge and flapjacks with sweet syrup in the connected tavern, she was ready to continue. Her reindeer had been fed and watered in the inn's stable overnight, so it was as ready to continue as Keyt was. Mysterious lands waited beyond the next vineyard-covered hill, lands that were filled with promise and hopefully contained the water she sought. Or, if nothing else, they would hopefully hold more information about the spring itself.

The trip from Dian to Rex, the closest moderately-sized town within the Dracott Empire, took much longer than she had expected. Muddy rain fell from the sky, drenching her in filth. She had never seen such an occurrence, as back home the water fell clear and clean. Here, on the other hand, it seemed as though dirt generated from the falling rain itself, deposited on the ground as it landed. Keyt had never seen such an occurrence and wasn't sure what to make of the phenomenon. Was it natural, or some sort of message from the gods? Did this land have its own blight, one unfamiliar to her?

When the rains finally stopped, the clouds parted to reveal the bright, familiar sun high in the sky. The sun, in its turn, baked and dried the mud on her clothing until she could pluck at it, peeling it away in sheets. The first time she came across a stream that appeared relatively clean, she spent over an hour bathing herself, her reindeer, and her clothes, trying to get the mess out of the cloth, off her skin, and out of her hair. The water ran dark with the accumulated grime, but she felt a lot better. Perhaps not exactly clean, but definitely better.

When she finally spotted a town in the distance, she sighed in relief. "No wonder mother didn't bother coming this way," she told the reindeer. "If this is what the roads are like all the way through the Dracott Empire, it makes me wonder how they get anything done at all." Despite the hot sun overhead and her attempts to clean the caked mud from them both, its hooves had become re-coated with the thick muck almost immediately, proving time and time again how futile her efforts were. They had stopped a few times since then to scrape the grime away but it hardly mattered. As though it understood her, the reindeer snorted in response.

She had developed a habit, years previously, of talking to the reindeer. Not having very many friends back home, her only options for conversation were her mother, her brother, or the reindeer. She had felt badly any time she brought her problems to her mother, knowing that the older woman had far more important things to deal with than Keyt's daily mishaps, thoughts, and observations. Malec tried to help but his own frailty and assortment of health issues often made such impossible, as he was sick abed more often than not. So she had resorted to speaking to the reindeer and other livestock, often feeling better after discussing her problems with them. Their solemn silence was comforting, a comfort she had needed many times throughout the years.

"I think this is going to be the last leg of the trip for you, my friend." She reached forward and petted the soft fur between her mount's antlers. "The weather is much warmer and far wetter out here than it was back home, soon it will be a bad place for you to be."

She considered selling the reindeer immediately once she arrived in town, but one glance around informed her that it wouldn't be a wise decision quite yet. Urchins littered the streets, homeless children begging for a thaler or a crust of bread. Her heart went out to the pitiful creatures, but she continued on. She had no bread to share and while she had thalers, she couldn't be overly generous with them. Further in town, she spotted a gambling-house, a brothel, and other evidence that the town was closely intertwined with the local thieves' guild. "Perhaps more than one," she mused. "This many establishments must mean either one massive guild or multiple smaller ones."

She didn't have much experience with such guilds directly, but she had encountered them a few times previously. Once, years before, a handful of cutpurses had determined that her home town had been a good place to start their own guild. She remembered quite clearly the day the town's residents had taken up arms and rousted the thieves, running them out of town with plenty of warnings of what would come should they or their ilk decide to return. If any had taken up the challenge since, she hadn't heard of it.

For every disheartening thing she spotted as she walked slowly through the town, impressive features were revealed as well. Unlike the muddy pathway leading to the town, the streets upon which she walked were cobbled stone, the buildings in good repair. Many of the taverns and inns were bustling, particularly as she approached the shore. As she passed a bulletin board, she spotted a handful of notices and missives, some fresh and others obviously aged. One in particular caught her eye, a tattered warrant for someone known as the Dark Star. The notice explained that a reward of fifty tyros had been offered for his capture, a high bounty indeed. "Wonder what he's done to have such a price on his head," she commented as she continued her journey.

Rex was a truly sprawling city, easily the largest she had ever been to, and each one of its main streets led directly to the docks. The rest of the town spoked out from these primary lanes, like a gigantic wheel had been placed along the land, its shape traced to form the city. As she walked, she spotted a stable with horses for sale, just what she had been looking for. She approached, reins in hand, to see who was about.

"What's that you've got there?" A young man came forward to greet her. "A reindeer? How unusual. We haven't seen any of them around here lately."

"I've come from further north," Keyt explained. "The reindeer won't do well down here, so I was hoping you would be interested in purchasing him."

"Well, I'm not sure there's much of a demand for reindeer, but let's take a look, shall we?" He stepped forward to examine the reindeer, running his hands over its fur and examining its teeth. "Looks like he's in pretty good condition. How much you wanting for 'im?"

"Fifty tyros," she quoted him the normal selling price back home, not sure how much of a price difference there would be in Rex. The buck was still in perfect condition, if a bit in need of brushing after their journey together, so there was no reason to expect much of a price drop.

"Fifty?" The man whistled through his teeth. "That's a bit steep, particularly for one of these."

He leaned against the wall and looked from her to the reindeer and then back to her again. "Tell you what I'll do. I'll offer you twenty for 'im."

Keyt blinked in surprise. While she had expected the prices to be somewhat different in this foreign land, that was a substantial discount from what she had expected. Certain she was being swindled, she counteroffered. "I'll take forty."

When her offer wasn't rejected outright, she knew she was correct. The man leaned forward once more, examined the reindeer's antlers, and looked back up at her again. "I can do thirty-five, but that's the best I've got." He turned and spat into the grass, a disgusting stream of red-brown spittle. "Like you said, these aren't all that good out here, so I'll only be able to sell 'im if someone's wanting to travel north."

He had a valid point, so she accepted his offer. "I will accept thirty-five." Still sure that she was being underpaid for the beast, she watched as the man counted out the tyros. When he handed them over, she tucked them securely into her purse, noticing how many others around were watching with interest as she did so. Remembering the cutpurses who had invaded her home all those years ago, she decided that attaching her purse to her belt, where it had been hanging previously, would be folly. Instead, she tucked it more securely into the folds of her shirt. If any of the interested onlookers believed she would be a worthwhile target to steal from, she wasn't about to make it easy for them to do so.

She went directly to a nearby tavern, one with a placard hanging outside that announced itself to be the Drunken Sailor. It seemed appropriate, considering that the building had a direct line of sight to the docks and a good portion of its clientele appeared to be heavily intoxicated. "I imagine they get a lot of business," she thought as she looked around inside, "particularly when the merchants come in."

"Have a seat anywhere you like," a pretty young girl in a light blue skirt that reached to her ankles and a cream-colored shirt smiled at her. She was carrying a serving tray that was stacked high with plates and mugs of ale, all balanced precariously on one hand. Even as she spoke, she raised her other hand to steady the tipping tray.

"Thank you," Keyt responded remotely. While there were plenty of tables available, much smaller tables than the ones in the taverns back home, she selected out of habit the one furthest from the opening, away from the rest of the tavern's patrons. Almost before she had settled into her seat, a massive man in a stained white apron came to check on her.

"Hungry?" he asked. "Or just thirsty?" The man was far closer than those back home usually approached, his demeanor friendly and affable rather than cold and distant.

"Both," she replied. Of course the residents of Rex had no fear of her, she realized. They had probably never even heard of the Wasting, let alone have seen its effects. Even if they had heard of it, they would have no reason to suspect a connection between the woman in the tavern and the awful disease.

"Beer, ale, or mead?"

It had been a while since Keyt had gotten to enjoy a cup of mead, so she took its availability then as a welcome surprise. She also requested a bowl of the vegetable soup and a hunk of cured ham to go with it. "And bread," she added. "Please."

"Of course," the big man chuckled. "What good is a bowl of soup without some bread to dip in it?" His sky-blue eyes twinkled at her as he turned to leave. For as stout as the man was and considering how intimidating people that size could be, he was remarkably friendly and gracious and Keyt found herself warming to him immediately.

It only took a few moments for the meal and drink to arrive, both delivered by the girl who had greeted her. This time, all she carried was the tray with Keyt's order, nowhere near as difficult to balance as the last load had appeared to be. "If you need anything else," she said as she set down the cup, "don't hesitate to ask."

The soup and ale did little to soothe her aching muscles but did wonders to comfort her aching soul. The soup tasted very similar to that which Malec regularly made back home, filled with large chunks of potato and carrot and flavored with savory herbs, and she could almost see him with her at the table, dipping his own crust into the warm broth. The thoughts of him flooded through her, reinforcing her resolve to find an end to the horrid illness.

"You appear mighty troubled for one so young." The burly man's voice cut through her thoughts as he placed another hunk of bread onto her table. "Name's Harold. I've got a listening ear, if you've a need to talk."

Keyt wasn't sure why, but she felt comfortable with the man despite the amount of distance she usually kept from others. "I'm looking for something," she explained after introducing herself. "I heard tale of a spring whose waters could cure all ills." She looked up at the man before explaining. "It's my brother. I expect him to die soon, and I would greatly prefer he not."

Harold chuckled, pulled out a chair, and took a seat. "I expect most of us would prefer our brothers not die. What makes you believe yours will?"

"There's a family curse. It took our mother and now I fear it will take my brother as well." She explained about the Wasting, watching him carefully as she did. "Mother tried everything else to cure herself with no success, so this water may be the only hope he's got."

Harold nodded solemnly. "Sounds like you have quite the weight upon those shoulders." He looked at her thoughtfully for a moment before adding, "I was a bit of an explorer when I was young, oh how long ago that was! I had a loremaster traveling with me for a period of time. He once told me of a place where he and his fellow gatherers of knowledge would meet to share their stories, even recording them for future generations. Now, I don't know anything specific about this spring you're looking for, but if the story came from a loremaster, you may want to go to Sage's Island."

"Sage's Island?" She blinked at him. "I've not heard of this. Is it nearby?"

"Not overly close, no. It's a bit of a journey to get there, as I understand it. I've not been there, mind you, but plenty of others have. It's out toward the center of the Azul Sea, just about a week or so southeast of here."

Keyt groaned. The last thing she had expected was to need to travel by ship, which would be needed to get to an island in the center of the sea. Sure, ship travel was faster than walking or even taking a reindeer or horse along the road, but there had to be a better way of getting the information, wasn't there? "I don't suppose there are any places like that on land, are there?"

"Not that I know of," Harold chuckled. "But it's not as bad as all that. Plenty of traders go back and forth, most of which stop by here on the way to deliver supplies, so if you can find a ship headed in that direction, they'll probably as not be willing to take another passenger along with them."

"These people on Sage's Island, do you believe they'd be willing to share their information with me? I am hardly a loremaster."

"I have no idea," he shrugged. "As I said, I've never been there so I've never tried. But assuming that they are willing to share their knowledge with outsiders, that's the most likely place for you to find information on this spring."

6

Ship passage was a little more expensive than Keyt had anticipated. Luckily, she wasn't traveling very far and the pittance she had gained from the sale of the reindeer easily covered it. She had originally intended on spending the coins on a horse or other travelling beast, but that plan had dissolved as soon as she discovered where her next destination was. Horses were not well suited to overwater travel, so she would wait for such a purchase until the situation warranted it. After handing the promised payment to the shipmaster, she was assigned a small bunkroom, one with a bed and a desk as well as a small chest of drawers built into one wall beneath a small round porthole window.

"We can take you to Marisburgh," the captain had told her when she boarded, "that's the only port on Sage's Island we go to."

"How long will it take us to get there?" Although Harold had said a week or so, he had also indicated he wasn't entirely certain of the travel time and she wanted to know for how long she would be miserable.

"Eight days. Maybe ten, depending on the weather."

Keyt closed her eyes and steeled her spine. The week she had initially expected would have been bad enough, so hearing that there would be more time spent afloat was not wonderful news. Eight days on the creaky wooden firetrap sounded like eight days too many. Ten would be an absolute nightmare. Not only would ten days mean that she would spend an extra two days aboard, but that would also indicate that the seas would be rougher due to the weather the captain mentioned. The whole trip only sounded like misery compounded by misery, not to mention that she would need to repeat the trip to get back home again. She wasn't entirely sure how she was going to handle the trip there and she certainly didn't want to face the prospect of repeating it all over again. At least, not until she absolutely had to face it.

Her disappointment that neither Rex nor any of the towns on Sage's Island contained a portal had been great. While most travelers complained about the dizzying sensation of using one of the golden spheres, she much preferred to have a few moments of disorientation upon arrival to having multiple days of misery to achieve the same result. At least the misery caused by using the portal was over quickly and lasted a predictable amount of time. Ship travel, on the other hand, was nowhere near as swift or predictable.

This was hardly to be her first boat trip. As a young child, she had once accompanied her mother and brother on a trip to Vanguard, a journey they had made by boat. While most would attribute her lack of sustaining memories of the trip to her young age, she had always attributed it to the enduring sickness she had experienced from the trip there and back home again. Riding upon the water had not agreed with her then, nor had it agreed with her at any point since.

She stood upon the deck near the railing as the ship left port, watching as the peculiar city of Rex faded from view. The weather was clear, the drizzle of dirty rain that had greeted her arrival in the Dracott Empire had thankfully remained behind to continue assaulting the land. As the coastline, the borderline between solid ground and the unsteady planking she stood upon grew smaller and smaller, fading from view, replaced by an ever-increasing stretch of undulating water, she turned her attention to watch those working on the deck nearby.

Some men walked back and forth calmly, eyeing the rigging and checking the knotwork at the various hook points. Ropes were strung everywhere, some connected to beams or the ship itself, others connected only to more ropes. Other workers climbed up the sails, some using ladders made of more rope and others simply scaling the poles that held the fabric, adjusting the tension in them to catch the meager gusts of wind. Others grouped together to pull on heavy ropes, tugging the angle of sail to a more desirable position. All of them were sure-footed and ruddy-faced from years of experience. All of them worked in perfect concert, like the notes of a musical score, none interfering with the others and all in precisely the position that was needed to make the melody shine. She had never seen workers so in tune with each other without the need of a director, someone to monitor and call out orders. They had crafted this masterpiece themselves, each defining their own part and following it to the letter, none needing to be told how their performance impacted those around them.

"It's a nice view, isn't it?" one young man sidled up next to her. "I love this part, the hint of coastline at the very edge of vision, the smell of the salty air, the calls of the seabirds." He smiled out over the water.

"Yes," she agreed honestly. The view was lovely, particularly since the wave-sickness hadn't yet set in. "I can understand why you enjoy it so much." Had it not been for the knowledge of what was to come, she likely would have been enjoying it more herself as well.

"First trip?"

She turned her attention more directly to the boy. Upon closer inspection, he was a little younger than her initial impression had led her to believe, too tall to be a child but not quite filled out enough to be considered a man. He was likely closer to her own age than to Malec's. It may have been the glare from the sun reflecting off the water, but to her eyes, his hair was dark enough to resemble the midnight sky when no stars shone. "No. I've been on boats before. But I don't particularly enjoy them."

"Why not?"

"The seas," she explained, mimicking the rhythm of the waves with her hands. "My stomach doesn't appreciate them."

He nodded in comprehension, his eyes sympathetic. "I was like that at first, too. Spent my first week in bed because of it. But you get used to it eventually." He grinned again. "So much better than using a portal, that's for sure."

She smiled at him even though she didn't agree with his sentiment. It was one she often heard; one she didn't see any point in debating. Those who lived and worked upon the seas, even those who had experienced wave-sickness on their first time in open water, never understood why she didn't acclimate as others seemed to. That was a mystery to herself as well, one she didn't enjoy experiencing. If anything, she would need to spend a much longer time aboard a ship in order to overcome the sickness, time she had no intention of spending. Even had it not been for her current need for haste, she simply wasn't interested in doing such.

She continued to watch over the water as they sailed further out into the Azul Sea, wondering when the sickness would overcome her. While her muscles continued to ache from the first leg of her journey, she remained standing. It was just fatigue from unaccustomed activity, that was all. The muscles would calm eventually and the rest of her body would adjust, just as it did with any other activity to which it was unused. The fresh air would help to stave off the sickness for a time, as would the level view of the horizon. So long as the waves remained calm and land stayed within view, she should be fine.

As the sun climbed higher into the sky, the coastline faded from view completely and all she could see in any direction was wave upon wave upon wave. The horizon was no longer level and even, now it was a roiling mass of heaving water, the crest rising and falling with no discernible pattern. She closed her eyes against the familiar sensation, swallowing hard and dreading what she knew was to come next. The deck beneath her boots rose as the ship crested a large wave, then fell from beneath her as it crashed down the other side, sending a spray of salty water over the railing.

Having relieved herself of both breakfast and lunch, she retired to her cabin. The remainder of the trip would be spent in misery, but so long as she had water enough to drink and stave off the impending thirst, she should arrive reasonably whole. The only concern remaining to her was whether they would encounter any storms along the way. The current waves were bad enough, a storm would make everything much more so.

Keyt spent the next seven days in abject misery, primarily whiling away the time abed. She emptied her stomach of its contents time and time again, an activity that often left her weakened and light-headed, her throat and chest sore, raw from the effort. Had she been able to maintain any food in her stomach, allowing her something of substance to eject besides bile, she probably wouldn't have been quite as miserable, but the ceaseless motion of the sea ensured that was not to happen. A few times, the upheavals left her coughing and unable to catch her breath for a few long, frightening moments.

Jace, the same young-looking deckhand who had spoken with her the first day they had set to sail, came to check on her a few times during the trip, keeping her supplied with fresh water and bringing her tidbits to eat. "These should be easier for you to hold down," he explained as he held out a small dish of dried bread flakes. "We're going to be out for a while yet, so you need to keep something in you besides water."

Keyt accepted the offer but knew it would end up pointless. Her mother had offered her similar bread flakes on her first boat ride, which had proven quite useless. "Thank you," she said as she settled the bowl onto desk next to the bunk. Her voice was weak and tired from the time she had spent in her cabin, but that was no call for ignoring manners. "I appreciate your thoughtfulness."

Nights were somewhat better, as she was able to come out onto the deck for some fresh air. The moonlight didn't offer enough visibility to see the horizon, which helped. The boat also seemed to move slower at night, calmly bobbing through the water rather than crashing up and down the waves, as though resting for the frenetic activity of the next day. She slept fitfully during the daytime, fighting against her own digestive system at any point she was awake.

Early on the eighth day, just as she was about to retire to her room in preparation for the forthcoming sunrise and all of the sickness it brought with it, a call came down from high up on one of the masts. Curious, she stopped halfway across the deck to find out what was happening.

"Land," Jace explained. "We're close. The lookout's spotted land." He smiled at her. "You'll be back on solid ground soon enough. The trip's almost over."

Hope raising in her heart, Keyt turned back to the railing, leaning forward and peering into the distance. If land was nearby, that meant that her sickness had almost reached its end. Tired as she was from having spent the period of darkness awake, she was eager to bring the trip to a close, eager to see solid earth once more.

Just as slowly as it had faded from view, the coastline appeared. What had at first been nothing more than a shadow, a mirage fading in and out of view at the very edges of her vision grew into a more solid form. The early morning sun caused it to sparkle in the distance, a shimmer that she had initially believed to be nothing more than the endless waves she had already endured. As they drew closer, however, she began to spot the familiar signs of habitation, of life beyond the water. By late afternoon, she stepped off the gangplank and onto solid, unmoving ground once again. She was slightly unsteady on her feet, as though she had begun to acclimate to being on the waves, but soon she found her balance once more.

Every muscle in her body hurt from clenching against a week's worth of illness but she didn't care. Just as the soreness from her tired legs had passed, so too would the ache in her abdomen. The next portion of her journey would be taken on land, and that was all that mattered. The knowledge that the sickness she had just left behind also loomed ahead of her nestled in her brain, but she pushed the thoughts aside. She would deal with that when it arose, not a moment sooner. For now, she would simply enjoy the fact that the ground beneath her boots no longer moved.

In Marisburgh, she purchased an overnight stay at the first inn she spotted, thankful to be able to sleep without being tossed back and forth. The bunk was meager and hard, but anything at all would have been better than spending a single additional night on the ship. She was far more tired than she had been in a long while, both from the trip on the boat itself and from having been awake the entire night and a good portion of the day. Hungry as she may have been, sleep was far more important. She may have been asleep before the blanket settled entirely over her, but it didn't matter. So long as this bunk remained stationary.

The next morning, she went downstairs to the tavern, where she ate far more than she had been able over the entirety of the previous week. A plate of biscuits and sausages drenched in a thick, spicy gravy. A bowl of hearty porridge with strange orange flakes of cheese across the top. Slices of grilled bread drenched in a sweet sauce. Berries and sliced fruit accompanied everything. She ate until she could hardly consume another bite, and then ate just a few bites more.

The tavernmaid laughed as she saw the amount of food Keyt consumed. "I know that look," she explained at her curious glance. "You've just come from a boat."

"Is it that obvious?" Her words were slightly garbled as she fought to swallow the bite she had been chewing.

"Oh, yes. We see it all the time. Here." She settled a mug of steaming black brew in front of her. "This will help with the digestion."

The brew was rich and slightly bitter but as she took a second sip from the cup, Keyt could feel the liquid soothing her cramped stomach. She folded her hands around the cup, interlacing her fingers on the opposite side, and sighed in pleasure. This, she was certain, was assuredly a gift directly from the gods.

"So where are you headed?"

"I'm looking for the loremasters. I've been told they have a gathering place nearby."

The tavernmaid nodded. "I know the place. It's not here, though."

"No? Where is it?" She had expected to find her destination close by, so finding that it was not in Marisburgh was a disappointment. As long as she didn't have to board another boat to reach it, however, the disappointment was minimal.

"You're looking for Leavett. That's where the loremasters go to visit their library." She explained that the library in Leavett was the central area for all the amassed knowledge that the loremasters gathered. "All of the loremasters travel there about once a year or so to share their accumulated wisdom with their peers."

"That sounds like what I'm looking for." She took another drink of the steaming brew. "I suppose you see a lot of loremasters here, in that case."

The tavernmaid nodded and smiled more broadly. "Yep. Quite a few of them stop in here on their way to or from there. We get to know some of them from year to year."

"So how do I find Leavett? Is there a road?"

"There is a road, sure enough. Leavett's a few days' travel from here. But there are always plenty of caravans headed in that direction, so you should have no problem joining up with one of them."

7

The caravan that Keyt signed up with to make the trip from Marisburgh to Leavett was not scheduled to leave until the following morning, so Keyt spent a good portion of the day exploring the town. There wasn't a lot to be seen, despite the quantity of ships in the docks. From what she could tell, the town was more of a waystation on the trip to Leavett than anything more substantial than that. To her relief, they had a messenger shop, so she was able to send word home to Malec to reassure him that she was still doing well and that her journey was well underway. She explained in the message about the island she had landed upon and the boat ride she had taken to get there. Before sending it, she erased the last part of the message, not wanting Malec to worry about her health after such a ride.

He had been present for the first time she had been aboard a boat and well understood the effect that sea travel had on her. Better to let him think that she had traveled by portal, she decided.

To her surprise, she found a large fountain in the center of the town. Given how close the settlement was to the sea, she wouldn't have expected to find something so elaborate, so she stood back to watch the gurgling water in appreciation. The fountain itself wasn't anything overly fancy, a simple set of grey marble tiers with water dropping down from the highest level to the lowest basin. As she watched, a handful of children approached and scooped out handfuls to drink. At most, Keyt would have expected a simple well, so finding a freshwater fountain was a pleasant surprise. Maybe there was more to this strange little town than she had initially believed.

Soon, she found herself on a grassy slope overlooking the bay. There were quite a few boats docked in the bay, including the one she had arrived upon. A handful of seabirds circled high overhead, calling to each other, curious and apprehensive about the intruder. She paid the birds no mind, sitting down with her legs crossed before her and leaning forward, elbows on knees and chin in hands, to watch the clouds drift by in the distance. It was peaceful and serene, warm wind blowing gently across the hillside, bringing with it the mild tang of sea air layered with the pleasant scent of flowers. Fresh wild flowers, this time, with the underlying scents of animals and dirt, not the cloying, overwhelming flowers that had permeated the coffin maker's shop.

She pulled out her flute and played the song of the southern winds. It was the first song her mother had taught her, one that always brought forth the feeling of a warm summer breeze and at that moment, it felt the most appropriate. She played for her mother, who never got to see the island or make the trip across the sea. How Juleth would have loved to watch the clouds, gather the wild flowers, play in the fountain, and explore all of the promise of this new land. She played for her brother, in the hopes that the winds for which the song was named would somehow carry the tune to him. Her thoughts had been with Malec almost constantly since she had left him behind at home, wondering whether he was eating correctly and whether she would return in time for the nuptials that were surely coming up.

The song captured the attention of a handful of sailors nearby, who had been unloading goods and other supplies from their ship. They stopped to watch and listen in appreciation for a long moment before returning to work. Even the birds came closer to listen, curious as to the strange new noise in their habitat or perhaps feeling the same warm breeze that the music evoked for Keyt.

The light began to fade as the sun settled down for the night, pink-orange sky turning to deep blue and black, tiny twinkles of light appearing in the sky to replace the sun's diminishing glory. She flopped back onto the grass, looking up at the stars and marveling that they appeared so much the same as they had back home. Somehow, she had expected to see the distance she had traveled reflected in the night sky. But here they were the same, reassuring her that no matter how far she traveled, what she had to endure to get there, she was beneath the same canopy of stars as she had been back home. Surprising as that knowledge may have been, she also found it comforting. These were the same stars that had watched over her for her entire life, the same stars that still continued to watch over Malec.

The next morning, she was packed and ready to go when the caravan assembled. There were more wagons in the group than she had expected, with a large assortment of guards and merchants to go with them. A pair of heavily armored men with hand-held crossbows at the ready were stationed atop sturdy-looking horses at the front of the line of wagons. The horses were snorting at each other, pawing at the ground and dancing back and forth, obviously eager to get underway. The caravan master, a harried man in a long traveling cloak and large round glasses that continually slipped down over his sharply pointed nose scurried among the wagons, assigning passengers to their benches and ensuring that all of the merchants were properly cared for. She had already paid the caravan master for her passage, so once she received her own seat assignment, she placed her pack beneath the bench and settled in for the ride.

The caravan took almost as long to get from Marisburgh to Leavett as it had taken the ship to travel from Rex to Marisburgh, but Keyt didn't care. So long as she wasn't on a boat, solid on land, she was happy. She chatted amicably with some of the other passengers, surprised that none were loremasters on pilgrimage to the library. With everything she had been told so far, she had expected to see more of them traveling in this direction so for none of her fellow travelers to be on Sage's Island for that reason was unexpected.

One man in particular struck her as unusual among the group of travelers. He was friendly enough, she supposed, willing to chat mindlessly about anything and everything, but he seemed a bit too friendly for her tastes. The man was likely harmless, just lonely and seeking companionship along his own travels. Perhaps she had simply spent too much time on her own, she supposed. "Nice to meet you," he held out his hand in greeting. "You from Barberry?"

"I am," she agreed as she accepted his out-stretched hand. It wasn't a difficult guess, as the people from the northern lands of the Barberry Empire looked distinctly different than most in the southern lands. "Where are you from?"

"Little bit of here, little bit of there. Been all across the empires, but I originally started out in Dracott." He grinned and settled back on the bench, his vibrant blue eyes twinkling beneath dark brown hair. "Where you headed? I mean, obviously you're going to Leavett, but where from there?"

"Nowhere," she answered. "At least, nowhere that I know of quite yet."

"Meeting up with the loremasters there?" When she glanced over at him in surprise, he chuckled. "Well, that's about the only reason most of us travel there. Going to the same place myself. Probably the same for most of the people with us."

"I see." She tried to turn and watch the scenery as they rattled past, but he was not to be dismissed so easily.

"Looking for answers, or are you bringing new information?"

"Looking for answers, I suppose." Normally she wouldn't have hesitated to mention what she was actually after but something in the man's demeanor gave her pause. Something about their continued interaction led her to believe that her initial impression of him as being harmless had been false. There was something definitely cagey about this man. Had she spent more time among her peers, she likely would have had an easier time identifying what about the man was so off-putting, but she was unable. "Trying to find out more about my family. I understand they have a long history of lineages there."

The blue-eyed man nodded. "I see. Family's important." He tucked his thumbs into his belt and stretched. "Me, though, I've got other things I'm interested in. You familiar at all with the Inland Empire?"

"No," she shook her head. "Never been there." About the only interaction she had with the Inland Empire was the trip her mother had taken and the information that there was a loremaster somewhere within it that held the information that had started her on her quest. But there was no reason she saw to tell him about that, particularly since she had already decided not to tell this man about her quest at all.

"There's a town there, called Greystone. Really smart people there, coming up with all sorts of new inventions. But it's the old stuff I'm more interested in. Rumor tells that they've got a massive construct somewhere that's been lost for ages."

"Construct?" She blinked uncomprehendingly. "What kind of construct?"

"See, that's the thing. Nobody knows. Might be something useful, might be something less useful. Only way to find out is to find it and see what it can do."

"So that's what you're looking for? Information about this lost construct?"

"Yep, that's it. I want to know what it is, why they built it, and what it can do. Hopefully, I can figure out how to control the thing too."

He continued to babble away about the mysterious construct that may or may not even exist for a while before a pretty merchant girl caught his eye. "You take care," he said as he stood to leave. "Maybe we'll run into each other again someday."

Once he was gone, Keyt settled herself back down and closed her eyes, hoping that she wouldn't have to deal with much more conversation along the trip. While she didn't object to the occasional discussion with other people, she was uncomfortable doing such for lengthy periods of time. The amount of energy just to maintain the conversation with the strange man had been exhausting. The novelty of having people unafraid to approach her, sparking conversations that she was ill-equipped to carry forward, was quickly beginning to lose some of its luster. While she continued to appreciate the lack of fear, she missed the quiet and solitude her previous life had guaranteed.

Leavett was a large city on the shores of Sage's Cove, with plenty of shipping space for arrivals. Not only was the town itself much larger than Marisburgh or even Rex had been, the docks that stretched out into the cove were truly massive.

Row upon row upon row of slips, waiting for ships to arrive, grew like an ever-reproducing plant into the sea. The ground beyond the docks was striped in sunlight and shade, cast by massive aqueducts high overhead that carried water from one end of town to the other, supported at regular intervals by massive stone pillars.

When the caravan stopped in the shade of one of these pillars, the caravan master immediately began dashing from wagon to wagon, needlessly informing everyone that they had arrived. Keyt gathered her belongings and headed toward the largest building in view, an enormous sign in front of which announced it to be the library she sought. Just ahead of her, she spotted the dark-haired man who had spoken with her along the way. Thankfully, he didn't seem to notice her, and she felt no need whatsoever to remind him of her presence now. Silently, she shouldered her pack and trudged along the pathway leading from the cobbled street to the library entrance, deliberately slowing her pace to allow more room between the man's entry and her own. Once he disappeared into the massive building and pleased to finally have reached the end of this leg of her journey, she hitched her bag more securely onto her shoulder and headed inside.

"Greetings, fellow seeker of knowledge," an elderly man scuttled over to meet her almost the second her foot crossed the threshold. "To what may we attribute your presence with us today?" Wire-framed spectacles dangled around his neck by a thin, fine chain.

The building itself was clean and spacious, with blue and grey marble floors underfoot and the scent of aged parchment hanging in the air. An assortment of tables was lined up near the entryway, each with a carved wooden chair along each side. Beyond the tables were orderly rows of shelves leading deeper into the library, each of which was piled high with books, scrolls, stone tablets, sheets of parchment, and other various items. Light beamed in through a large arched skylight at the top of the building as well as a row of glass panels that lined one wall, offering a beautiful view of the Azul Sea. A quick glance around reassured her that the talkative man who had entered before her was no longer in sight.

"I'm looking for information." The man who had greeted her was only half her own height, so Keyt tried to not tower over him overly much as she looked down to meet the man's eyes.

"If information is what you desire, you have come to the correct place indeed. My name is Bazik and I will endeavor to assist you in any way I can. For here within these hallowed walls can be found all the knowledge you could ever hope to find." He swept an arm out grandly as he spoke, bringing it in and lowering his voice conspiratorially as he added, "even, perhaps, some that you may not have known you needed."

She blinked at the strange man in confusion, not quite understanding what he was talking about and then looked up at the oppressive rows of shelves. "I'm trying to find information on a magical spring. One that can be used to heal any manner of ill."

Now it was Bazik's turn to register surprise, the wrinkles on his forehead multiplying as his eyebrows lifted. "You seek the lifespring? That is unusual, unusual indeed!"

"Why is that so unusual? Plenty of others have heard of this spring, as I understand it." She had hardly expected to be the first to come to the library to find out what they knew of the magical spring.

"That is true," Bazik nodded. "We get a great many reports of the lifespring, but very few come in search of it." Slowly his features settled back into their original position.

His words encouraged her, as many reports meant that there had to be something useful for her quest, some nugget of information that would tell her in which direction she needed to head. She brightened considerably as hope grew within her. "Can you help me find the information I need?"

"I can, of course. Come with me." He turned to lead her further into the building. "You must realize the dangers in seeking the lifespring. What, if I may ask, brings you on this quest?"

"Dangers?" She hadn't heard anything about the search being dangerous, other than the natural dangers of travel. Was this why few came in search of it?

"Why, yes. Hadn't you heard? Most who seek the lifespring never find it. Often, they fall victim to the perils of the search."

That didn't sound so bad. In fact, it sounded perfectly reasonable to her ears. Going in search of a mythical spring was obviously a gamble and the odds of finding it were slim at best, and there were dangers along any journey into uncharted and therefore unknown places. "You said most. I expect that means that others have found it?" Of course the lifespring, as he had called it, would not be found somewhere heavily trafficked, else it would have become common knowledge already.

"Of course, of course." He looked thoughtful for a moment before adding, "of course, none in a very long time."

"Then it seems like it would be worth the attempt, if it was needed badly enough."

"Needed badly enough? Well now, there's an interesting thought."

Even more confused than she had been at the beginning of the conversation, and equally lost in the maze of shelves and tables, she stopped. "Why is that an interesting thought? Why would someone search for something like this, particularly if it is so dangerous, if it wasn't badly needed?"

"Why, for life, of course. The lifespring doesn't just cure all ills, you know."

His answer did little to quell her confusion. "No. I hadn't known. What else does it do?"

"It is said that the lifespring is called such because it is the source of life itself. When one drinks of the source of life, one ceases to be subjected to its end." He stopped at another row of books. "We are almost there. Come along, now."

Sighing, Keyt followed. Bazik had obviously spent far too much time locked away in the library instead of out among people, conversing with him was every bit as unfathomable as the endless shelves they walked past. She recognized the parallels between that thought and her own secluded existence and wondered if she seemed as strange to others as Bazik seemed to her. She really hoped not. "It sounds as though that is the whole point, is it not? To drink from the water, the lifespring, means that you aren't sick anymore so of course you won't die."

"Ah, here we are." He pulled a handful of books and scrolls from a high shelf and deposited them onto a nearby table for her. "And you are correct, of course. Those who drink of the spring are no longer ill. But that is only the beginning."

She looked in dismay at the growing pile of materials on the table. "Are all of these about the lifespring?" How was she ever going to get through this stack and find the information she needed? A stack this large would take weeks, if not months, to go through.

"All of these contain information about the lifespring, yes. However, not all of these are solely about the spring you seek."

"What do you mean about that only being the beginning?"

Bazik had already turned back to perusing the shelves once again. "Hmm? Oh, yes, of course. By drinking of the lifespring, one is healed of all manner of ills. I do not believe that there is any known ill that the lifespring cannot cure. But you must be aware, the healing of ills is only a very small portion of what the lifespring can do." When she looked at him in silent confusion, he raised his spectacles and placed them onto his nose before continuing. "Death itself, you see, is one of the ills it halts."

Dawning set in. "When you said that those who drink the water are not subject to life's end, you meant that they just don't die. Not from whatever had ailed them to begin with, but not by any reason at all?" The very idea sounded incredulous. How could anyone live continuously without dying?

"Of course. That is the true power of the lifespring. It grants endless life." His tone indicated that the statement should have been obvious.

She sank into a chair, stunned. It hadn't been obvious at all. It hadn't even been something she had considered. How could such a thing be real?

Bazik sighed and turned to her more fully. He lowered his spectacles once more, letting them rest against his small chest. "I can see that you are not here seeking eternal life. That can only mean that you seek to be cured of the incurable."

"It's for my brother," she whispered. "He will die if I do not find a means of saving him."

"I see." His brows raised in sympathy. "Nothing motivates more, nothing is more worth saving, than one's family. Were the clerics unable to help with this illness of his?"

Keyt shook her head. "It's a family curse, one that took our mother not long ago. Now, it appears that my brother will be the next to die." She explained about how her mother had already traveled extensively in the hopes of finding a cure, how Malec had always been sickly, even as a child, and finally about her own worries that he wouldn't live very long. "So this is truly is the last option we have."

"Well," he put his spectacles back onto his nose once more and turned back to the assortment of documents on the table. "Each of these has at least one report of a magical, life-restoring spring, so I am certain that if the true location of the lifespring is to be found, it will be found somewhere in here." When she didn't immediately join him in rifling through the stack, he looked back up at her. "Is there something else amiss?"

"I'm not sure whether it's amiss or not," she explained, "but I'm not sure that waters granting immortality are the best way to go right now. I hadn't realized that was one of its properties until I came here." She stepped forward and began perusing the materials half-heartedly. "Do any of these describe springs that heal without immortality?"

Bazik looked thoughtful for a moment. "None of which I am aware," he admitted finally. "Does immortality not appeal to you? That is usually the reason people go in search of springs like these."

She shook her head. "I don't want to live forever and I strongly doubt Malec does either." In truth, she found the idea to be the most horrifying thing she could imagine. To live forever, watching those around you pass, seeing the world in which you had once lived change into something unrecognizable, sounded like a fate worse by far than the Wasting. If she had to choose between eternal life and dying from the family curse, she would choose the curse. She was sure her brother would feel the same way.

Perhaps that was the true extent of her family's curse, the choice between living forever and dying, being forced to make such an awful decision.

How could the gods be so cruel? To have a cure dangled before her, a hint of salvation, only to have it snatched away again. The rush of hope she had felt the first day she had overheard the conversation about a magical spring played back again in her mind, this time soured by the new knowledge she had gained. This was no hope, this was no cure. This was nothing more than yet another trick played upon her family by the cruel whims of the gods.

"Perhaps there is an additional solution to your problem," Bazik offered. "If a skilled alchemist was to process the water, they may be able to transform it to act as a curative instead of an immortality potion."

"That is an idea," she agreed. While Juleth had been to see many alchemists, none had already possessed such a curative. Perhaps, she considered, that was only because they lacked the life-spring water.

"The means by which the water is administered may alter its effects as well," Bazik continued. "For example, by bathing in it rather than drinking it, different effects may be applied. This could considerably lessen the water's effects, possibly even to the point where the bather is not immortal but instead becomes healthy."

They discussed the options further, continuing to dig through the records all the while. Slowly, the soured hope began to clear up in Keyt's mind once more as options expanded before her yet again. Finally, they decided that the best means to end up with the curative she needed was to find an alchemist. "Preferably," Bazik explained, "one trained also in the arts of necromancy."

"Necromancy?" Keyt recoiled at the word. "Why would they need to be trained in necromancy?" While she had never known a necromancer in her life, she had heard plenty of stories about them and the horrid acts of which they were capable. Killing at a single touch, turning people into soulless slaves, even raising the dead to fight in vast numbers, entire armies filled with corpses. All of those were things necromancers were known to do, saving lives was most definitely not among them.

"Because necromancers aren't all the evil people you have so obviously heard them to be. They are simply specialists in the borderlands between life and death." He finished transcribing the passages from the final scroll and handed it over to her. "Which, unless I am mistaken, is precisely what you are looking for, is it not?"

8

Once she had the copies Bazik made for her in hand, Keyt headed for a local tavern. Not only could she use a meal, but she could also use a pint or two of ale. Where she had expected to find one record of the magical spring, perhaps even two or three, much more than that had been uncovered at the library. There were a lot more pages than she had expected, most of which only referenced the lifespring in passing but many others that described the spring in greater detail.

These descriptions heartened her until she read through them more closely. Each of them seemed to describe a different spring, all in different locations scattered around the four empires. Some of them she discarded almost immediately, knowing that there was no such spring in Vanguard, nor was she willing to believe in the information about summoning the spring on a moonless night after sacrificing an assortment of expensive trinkets. She didn't want fables and she certainly didn't want a magical spell that would do nothing greater than to cost her even more of her savings than what she had already spent.

"Lifespring, hmm?" The most ancient man she had ever seen peered over her shoulder, leaning closely enough to see what she was looking at but not closely enough to make contact. "That's an interestin' thing for a lass like yerself to be readin'." Without waiting for invitation, he settled himself at her table, sighing heavily as he lowered himself into the seat. "Not sure you want to be hunting that," he clucked his tongue disapprovingly. "Bad luck, that's what it is."

"Bad luck?" She looked over at the strange man curiously. She wasn't concerned about him joining her, despite the selection of empty tables at which he could have sat. Back home, it was far less polite to sit aside from others than it was to join them without invitation. Unless you were a member of her cursed family, of course. They were expected to sit apart from others when possible. "Why is it bad luck?"

"Why?" He signaled for a meal and an ale to be brought for him and then leaned forward conspiratorially, arms crossed at the wrist on the table in front of him. "Because, you see," he lifted the index finger of his top hand to gesture slightly, "people who go hunting for things like that tend to find 'em." He lowered his finger and leaned back once more. "Either that, or they die tryin'."

"You're referencing the immortality portion of the spring." It wasn't a question, just an assumption on her part.

"Yep," he grinned at her. "Immortality sounds good an' all, but you can sure 'nuff take it from me, living is one thing but stayin' young is a completely differen' thing."

She blinked slowly at him, accepting her meal when it arrived. "I can see why you would say that, considering how long you have lived."

He guffawed at her words, for reasons that weren't entirely clear to her. "Yep, I be older 'n most, that's for certain." He accepted his own plate of food, glancing appreciatively at the young woman who delivered it. To his credit, the glance was all he did before turning to his meal. "Seen lots o' life in my years. Lots o' death, too."

"Are you a loremaster?" Normally the question wouldn't have occurred to her but when she considered where she currently sat, in the heart of the loremasters' world, the thought made sense. If this man was a loremaster, as she believed, he had likely seen far more of the four kingdoms than most of the others had.

"Ayuh," he agreed. "Been one for nigh on forty years now." He took a deep swig of his ale and sighed contentedly. "Nowhere near as good as the stuff from Greystone," he explained as he returned the tankard to the table, "but much better than in lots o' other places I been."

"Then maybe you would be so kind as to help me."

"Now why would I want to do that? Like I says, the lifespring's nothin' but bad luck. You'd do far better to steer clear o' that."

"If it matters at all," she explained, "I'm not seeking immortality. Personally, I agree with you that living forever sounds terrible."

"Then why are you lookin' for it?" He raised his mug and took another drink, eyes focused on her as he did.

"I'm seeking a cure for my family's curse before it kills my brother."

He eyed her for a moment at her explanation, as though trying to determine how much of what she said was true. Finally, he set the tankard back onto the table and leaned forward once more. "Family curse?"

"Yes. My family has been cursed by a disease called the Wasting for many generations. My mother passed of it not long ago and my brother is sure to follow her before too long."

"Wasting, hmm?" he looked from her to the papers and then back to her once more. "You from up in the Barberry Empire?"

"I am."

He nodded. "Thought as much. I heard somethin' a while back, about a family of outcasts up north. Somethin' about 'em all having this strange disease that took 'em all while they were young."

"You don't look afraid."

"Why would I be?"

"Most are," she shrugged. "Even though I don't have any signs of it, people assume I do because my mother did. They avoid us because they don't want to catch it, as though it could be passed from us to them just by being too close to one of us."

"Sounds lonely."

"Lonely? How would I know?" She took a drink of her own ale. "It's the only life I've ever known."

"That why you're sittin' over here by yerself?"

"I suppose."

"Ye wed?"

She shook her head. "The Wasting passes from the mother. Even if I don't have it, I can still pass it to my children, should I have some. I decided long ago that I wouldn't do that."

"What about yer brother?"

"He has a lady. He's afraid to wed for fear of the Wasting passing from him. He knows that it's not possible, but he worries nevertheless."

"So you want yer brother to have the life you couldn't? Since you can't have a family of your own?" Somewhere during the conversation, his voice had turned gentle, as though he understood the pain that her family accepted as daily life.

Keyt nodded. "All he needs to do is live. But he already has the Wasting, so he is not long for this world."

"So how will you keep yer brother from livin' forever? Even if you do find the lifespring, how to you expect to get the healin' without the rest?"

"Death mage," she explained. "If I can locate a necromancer who knows alchemy, they may be able to dilute the water so that it can cure him without the lasting effects."

He raised an eyebrow. "That might work. Where d'ye think yer gonna find one o' those?"

"I have no idea. To be honest, I'm not sure such a person exists." She smiled wryly. "Why would a death mage spend the time to learn alchemy?" She took another bite of her meal. "But then, I'm also not entirely sure the lifespring exists, either."

"Lemme see those." He reached out and pulled the pages closer to him so that he could read them. He immediately dropped a handful of pages off to the side. "These're all junk," he explained. "There's nothing worth findin' in any o' these places." By the time he was done scanning the papers, only three potential locations remained. "I can't tell you for sure," he said as he slid the pages back in front of her, "but if the lifespring really does exist, it's at one o' these places."

"Thanks," she said appreciatively as she looked through the papers. From over a dozen possible sites, he had narrowed it down to just three. One location was in the Fusite desert, one in the Ram Mountains, and a third was in the subterranean caverns near Ruschlack Lake. Both the desert and the mountains were nearby in the Sapphire Empire to the south and Ruschlack Lake was further north in the Dracott Empire. So long as one of them held what she needed, it was a drastic improvement. "This is wonderful, thanks so much."

"Not to worry," the old man said as he stood to leave. "An' when it comes time to find yer alchemist, I'd suggest checking a place called Dragon Keep. It's in the Inland Empire, but easy enough to get to. There's a gate system being set up out thaddaways, one that'll get you there faster 'n a cart any day."

9

The very tip of the Ram Mountains, directly to the east and slightly south of Sage's Island, could just barely be seen from Leavett on a clear day. The snow-capped mountain range soared into the sky, high enough that even the clouds moved of its way as they passed. The mountain range was the most predominant feature of the empire and its capital city, also named Sapphire, was at the northernmost tip of the range. Since that was the closest destination by far among her three options, Keyt decided to start the second leg of her search there. From the mountain, it would be easy enough to cross the range and head toward the Fusite Desert. Once she finished her journey in the desert, she could figure out how to get to Ruschlack.

Once again lamenting the fact that no portal was available in Leavett, she reluctantly booked passage on another ship, this time heading toward Canns. On the one hand, she would have liked to arrive closer to the mountains, lessening her journey once back on land once more, but she knew that any added length of time aboard the ship would be nothing short of torturous. Canns was the closest port to Sage's Island and the least offensive route she could take.

"Why can't these people just put in a portal?" she grumbled, more to herself than to anyone else. "I mean really, who heard of an entire island like this, one with multiple cities on it and a destination for troves of people to not have a portal?" The time away from home, not knowing what was going on with Malec had caused her to become irritable. It wasn't rational, but it was still there. A small part of her resented the fact that while she sent him regular updates, informing him of where she was and assuring him that she was okay, he couldn't send her the same. There was simply no way to know whether he was taking care of himself, whether he and Leoni had already married or if they were waiting for something. She hoped that if they were waiting, they weren't waiting for her return. But it would be nice to know that he was okay and that she hadn't undertaken this journey for nothing.

"They did that on purpose," one of the residents offered. "Originally, this place was supposed to be kept secret, hidden away from prying eyes, so that it could hold and keep safe all of the gathered knowledge. Once word started to spread, they decided to open the library so that anyone who needed information on something could come by and get what they needed, but they didn't want the trip here to be an easy one, such as walking through a portal. Taking a ship to get here hearkens back to the older days when loremasters would make the journey here in secret."

Keyt thought the idea sounded ridiculous, but she was no one to judge. In her opinion, once they opened the area up to everyone, particularly when more towns started popping up specifically due to the influx of travelers, they should have made the whole place much easier to access. If they were that against putting in a portal at

Leavett, they could at least put one in Maris-burgh. Or even, she supposed, Brownsville on the opposite side of the island from Marisburgh. There were plenty of other small towns to choose from on Sage's Island too, ones that could easily support a portal.

On the other hand, she could understand the desire to stick with tradition. Goodness knew, her own homeland had plenty of those as well. However, most of their traditions had risen out of a need, specialized for the harsh northlands. Tradition be damned, nobody in their right mind would suggest that they should make traveling through the Barberry Empire any harder than it already was. Had anyone tried to suggest such a thing, they would have been met with scorn at best, swords at worst.

Large mountains in the distance are decep-tive, and Keyt should have known better. She had made the mistake of believing that because she could see the mountain range from Sage's Island, which was an indicator that the two were close together. She couldn't have been more wrong had she tried. Had she taken the time to actually find out anything about the distances involved, she would have expected the trip to Canns to take about two weeks. That meant that the time spent on the boat from the island was not shorter than the arriving journey. To the contrary, it was even longer than the trip to the island had been. Keyt spent the majority of her time either lying on her bunk wishing she had the ability to teleport, or at least the ability to heal the sickness that overcame her on every boat ride, or at the railing above decks, offering the water gods all of the meals she managed to consume along the way.

Unlike her trip to Sage's Island, the journey to Canns was beset by a storm, not one strong enough to capsize or even truly threaten the ship but more than enough to keep her belowdecks for most of the trip. Even without seeing the boiling seas, there was no mistaking the wildly pitching world around her or the thunderous drumbeat of rain on the walls next to where she tried in vain to sleep. The skies had darkened, turning into a bruised wound stretching from horizon to horizon and the storm cried in matching anguish to her own.

"Miss?" One of the sailors came to check on her. "Do we need to bring down the cleric?" As with many boats, this one had a cleric on board. Not a powerful one, of course, but one strong enough to heal the minor injuries that were often sustained along such journeys. It was also beneficial, she was sure, to have someone on board who could curry favor with the gods. She did have to question whether this particular cleric had forgotten to tithe to the storm gods or whether his offering had simply been rejected.

"No," she groaned as the boat dropped on the far side of yet another of the seemingly endless chain of swells. "I'll be fine once the room stops moving."

"Okay," the sailor grudgingly accepted. "But if you don't get better soon, I'll bring him down anyway."

When two more days passed with no improvement from her, due in no small part to the lack of improvement in the weather, the sailor made good on his promise, coming to her door yet again to bother her, this time with a second man in tow. The cleric alleviated her sickness somewhat, nowhere near enough to make her feel good but enough to allow her a meal and some water before being overcome yet again. In her weakened state, there was little she could do to thank them; she simply hoped that her pitiful whimpering conveyed the message.

Would she ever escape from this vile water torture? She was beginning to have doubts. Perhaps at some point she had perished without realization and this was the punishment meted out in the next life. Solid, unmoving ground was quickly becoming a distant memory; her world was filled with ghastly rocking, clenched stomach muscles, and a foul tase that water could no longer wash from her tongue.

When she finally reached land once more, she was even more miserable than she had expected to be. Although the cleric had been by a few times along the trip, each time granting her a small window of relief from the water-sickness, the illness always resumed and she had found herself curled up on her bunk once more, wondering if perhaps death would be preferrable after all. Only thoughts of her dear brother Malec, waiting anxiously for her return, kept her looking forward. While she was undernourished from the trip, even the thought of food turned her stomach so she waited for a full day before seeking a meal. For two days after arriving in Canns, she stayed in her room at the inn, curled up and sleeping.

Thankfully, the inn didn't move around nearly as much as the ship had done. It was blessedly stationary.

Once she was rested and feeling a bit better, having finally kept down a full meal, she got her first good look at her next destination. Although she had spotted the mountains from Sage's Island and had caught the occasional glimpse of them from the ship on the handful of times she had been on deck, this was the closest view she had gotten of them so far. The Ram Mountains, which appeared in no way that she could see to resemble a ram, rose high overhead, an impressive mass even at the distance away from it she still was.

Distances, as she well knew, could be deceiving as objects far away such as the mountain range could be much larger and therefore much further away than she initially suspected them to be. It was the same illusion that had led her to believe the trip from Sage's Island to be a short one, a mistake she would not quickly make again. Even so, the papers she still carried with her, documents she had brought from the library, meant she had a decent idea of where in the mountains she needed to look. Now she just needed to figure out how to get there.

That afternoon, she went in search of maps of the local area. Trade routes, she was sure, had to cross the mountain, as it was simply inconceivable that they would travel all the way around the mountains just to reverse course and arrive a short distance away from where they had started. That knowledge necessitated that there must be a pass somewhere, in a place she had not yet identified. The traders near the mountain range simply had to have a way to pass to the other side without having to encircle it.

Furthermore, she couldn't imagine that a loremaster, even a very brave one, had gone too far up the mountain and away from everything else that could grant easy access to and from a nearby town unless they had used one of the passes. To do anything otherwise was foolhardy at best, potentially lethal at worst. Therefore, finding the passes over the mountain would be her next goal. From there she could determine which was the best to follow in her search.

"Looking for something in particular, miss?" She was getting used to being called miss. While the name wasn't one with which she was familiar, it was the default greeting by which strangers often addressed her in these strange southern lands. Not just her, she had quickly learned, but it was used to address all women whose names they didn't know. The young man helping her to sort through scroll after scroll of maps was no different.

"I'm looking for a map that shows the passes over the Ram Mountains," she explained. "I believe that what I am looking for is somewhere near one of them, so I need to know how many there are in order to figure out which one I need to take."

"Looking for the pass routes, hmm?" He turned and began to rummage through a different pile of rolled maps. "I've got a few of those over here, might have what you're looking for in them." He set a handful of scrolls on the table and held the corners as she began unrolling them one after another. "Passes are dangerous during the coldest part of the year, so if you're going to travel through one of them, best to leave soon before they get all snowed in and you find yourself stuck."

Keyt was well aware of the dangers traveling in snow-laden landscapes, so she simply smiled at the young man. "I'm aware. But I don't intend to spend any more time up there than absolutely necessary, so it should be safe enough as long as I start up before high summer is over."

The third scroll from the latest pile appeared to have what she sought. Not only did it show all of the passes but it also showed some of the other landmark features, such as the treeline and some of the vertical cliff-faces that couldn't be spotted from the base of the mountain. More importantly, it showed a number of the waterways on both sides of the range. Just a quick perusal confirmed her initial glance. It was perfect. "I'll take this one," she said. "How much?"

"That one? Four thalers."

The price was more than reasonable so she wasted no time counting out the copper coins and tucking the map scroll securely into her bag, nestling it alongside the papers she had gotten from the library. While she hadn't spotted precisely what she needed on the map, it had enough detail that she should be able to figure out where to go from the available information.

"Anything else I can help you with?"

"No, this is all I need. Thank you for your assistance." Without giving the boy a chance to sell her something she neither needed nor wanted, she turned and left the shop. Not that she would blame him for trying, everyone had to make a living, after all and selling items from the store was how he made his. She just wasn't in the mood to deal with it.

Her next stop was the tavern next to her inn. It had reasonable food and inexpensive beer, although none of the ales she would have preferred and no mead whatsoever. Although she didn't need to hide away from the rest of the patrons as she would have been expected to back home, she still took a small table away from the bulk of the seating. At least there, she could peruse the map further without worrying overmuch about interruptions. She would have preferred to do such with a mug of mead from the northern lands, though.

She began to trace the waterways, starting by identifying all of them that appeared to be in the general area she needed. Many of the streams appeared to converge a few days' trek away from the peak of the pass, which was a relief. Skilled as she was at hiking in the ice and snow, she wasn't sure as to how much different the snows on the mountains would be from the snows with which she was more familiar back home. One thing that nobody from the Barberry Empire would ever underestimate was the danger inherent in snow cover. It hid anything that may be hiding beneath the white blanket, from open pits to jagged rocks to all manner of things between.

"I'm going to need better climbing gear," she decided finally. While she had some specialized gear for maneuvering through the deepest of snow and other gear to assist climbing mountains similar to the one she now faced, both sets of gear were safely stored back home. "Why did I not bring them with me?" she lamented.

When the serving girl came over to check on her and see whether she wanted another beer, she agreed to the refill. Although she had initially expected nothing more interesting than a standard beer, she had been pleasantly surprised to discover that it was anything but. "Where does this come from?" she asked the server as the glass was refilled.

"It's good, isn't it? We're the only ones around here who have this kind. One of our brewers makes it especially for us." She leaned closer, uncomfortably so, to whisper, "it's the figs he grows on the mountain that make it so delicious."

Fig beer? Keyt had never heard of such a thing. But the girl was right, the beer was delicious. "Is there anywhere around here to get mountain equipment?" she asked. "Specifically, mountain climbing gear."

"We have a shop here in town, just to the north of here," the girl offered, "but as to whether it has what you need depends on how far up the mountain you intend to go. It primarily has just the standard equipment for climbing near the base of the mountain, but nothing for climbing much higher than the foothills."

Keyt's mouth twisted to the side. "I plan to go fairly high, just beyond the peak of the pass." Equipment designed for the low foothills wouldn't do at all for what she would need.

"In that case, you may want to check in Sapphire instead. They have much more climbing and snow equipment there. Both a better selection and, if I'm being honest, better prices too."

Keyt raised an eyebrow and cocked her head slightly to the side at the girl's statement. "Why would you send me all the way to Sapphire?"

She shrugged in response. "Most of the people here, all the further they're interested in going up the mountain is to the higher foothills. We had a sapphire mine not too far away from here, that was what most of our supplies are geared for. If you want to go all the way up, though, the stuff we carry just won't cut it."

"I see." She looked down at the map once again. "You said Sapphire would have better goods?"

"Yes. Most who want to climb the mountains start there." She chuckled. "It's actually pretty rare for someone to want to climb the mountains from this area."

"How far away is Sapphire?" From the way the girl had spoken, it had sounded as though Sapphire was a large town, known to most people in the area. It was not one with which Keyt was familiar, other than its existence and that it was the capital city of the empire. She knew it was on the edge of the mountains somewhere but, from where she was, she couldn't tell precisely where she needed to go.

"It's up here." The serving girl reached out and pointed at a spot on Keyt's map. "At the tip of this peninsula here."

Keyt nodded slowly. "Well then," she picked up her mug of beer and took a drink, "I suppose

I will need to pick up some different supplies before I head out." From the distances displayed on her map, she estimated it would take about three weeks to make the journey from Canns to Sapphire but at least this time the trip could be made on foot. Perhaps, if she was lucky, she could find a caravan to join, which would be a bit faster still. The last thing she intended to do was to sail unless it became absolutely necessary to do so. The less time she had to spend on a boat, the better.

10

The journey from Canns to Sapphire ended up taking much less time than Keyt had expected. Rather than having to make the trek by foot, or even by caravan, she discovered that there was a new magical transportation device connected by something called a gate network in both towns.

"Sure enough, walking to Sapphire takes a long time," one of the shopkeepers confirmed as Keyt examined his wares, "but it'd be much faster to just use the gate network."

"Gate network?" She looked up from the shelves to meet his eyes directly. "I haven't heard of that. What is it?"

"New," he explained succinctly. "Just got put in not long ago. It works just like the big portals that have been around forever. These ones are a lot smaller and available in a lot more places. Doesn't cost as much neither."

"Does it work?" Magic was, by its very nature, mysterious and Keyt didn't hold a lot of faith in it, particularly where new magical devices were concerned. Portals, she was willing to trust. They had been around for a great many years and generation upon generation had used them to travel without incident. She had never even heard of a portal malfunctioning, so there was no reason to mistrust them. They did precisely what they were advertised to do, nothing more and nothing less. This new gate network did not have the same generations of use and therefore the same level of trust.

"Yep, we've been having people using them since the day it opened. Apparently they've been placed all over the Inland Empire and only recently started cropping up out here. Rumor has it, there's some up in Barberry now, too."

If what the shopkeeper said was true, that was wonderful news. The ability to travel instantaneously over long distances was an absolute blessing, particularly when going from one empire to another. She was still a bit skeptical about these new gates, but she was willing to put a little bit of faith in them. Anything that kept her from having to travel by boat was a godsend in her opinion. "You also said it cost less. How much does it cost to use?"

"A sheckel."

"Only a sheckel?" When compared to the tyro required to use the portal, that meant it was practically free. "Where is it?"

"North edge of town. Just head straight up this here road and you'll come right to it."

She thanked him and completed her purchase before heading up to check out the new gate. Before making any decisions, she needed to see it for herself, maybe even see how it worked for a bit before trying to use it.

It was right where the helpful shopkeeper had said it would be, a stonework archway with a small collection box placed against one side. The gate didn't look like much, nowhere near as impressive as the enormous golden spheres to which she was used and instead appearing more as an archway made of common-looking stone, possibly quarried directly from the mountains that loomed overhead. It didn't even have so much as an ounce of gold inlaid into the runes etched into its capstone. How could something so small, so plain, work effectively at all? Not for the first time, she questioned whether the information she had received from the shopkeeper was accurate. Wasn't all magical stuff supposed to be more decorated, more ornate?

A sign next to the gate explained what it was and how it was to be used, for which Keyt was grateful. Seeing and being told the basics of how the gate worked was all well and good, but nothing could beat a good, solid set of instructions. Particularly if those instructions were as easy to follow as these appeared to be. After reading the instructions carefully, she pulled a silver coin out of her purse and dropped it into the collection box. Instantly, she was overcome by the sensation of travel, similar to but less powerful than the feeling she got when using the portal. When the motion stopped and she opened her eyes, she found herself in a completely different place, standing just outside a gate identical to the one through which she had used in Canns.

Sapphire, the capital city of the Sapphire Empire, was absolutely massive. Even the largest city she had been to previously paled in comparison with the sheer size of the cliffside town. People of all races milled the streets, some on horseback others in wagons but most were on foot. Above the streets, buildings soared many stories into the sky, most only three or four but a handful more than even that impressive height. Rope and wood bridges connected some of the taller buildings, creating a secondary walkway for people to travel through the town. It seemed as though the city had grown until it reached capacity for the space it intended to occupy and then, rather than spawning off a new city, it had simply built another directly atop of the existing one.

She walked carefully through the streets, peering into storefront after storefront, amazed at the vast selection of items available for purchase. Grocers and general goods stores were to be found aplenty, as to be expected from a town this size. Armorers, blacksmiths, bladesmiths, and even the occasional silversmith distributed their wares proudly in storefront windows. She found a section of town that housed breeders of all manner of animal, from riding horses to pack mules to hunting birds to battle cats. Unsurprisingly, there were no reindeer breeders. That was to be expected, as the climate in the Sapphire Empire was far too warm for the beasts.

The storefronts were not the only available attraction in Sapphire. Temples and places of worship dedicated to every god she had ever heard of, as well as many she had not, could be found everywhere. Restaurants invited from every streetcorner, many of which specialized in traditional foods from one specific area or another. Keyt was surprised to see that even foods local to the Barberry Empire could be found and she immediately went inside for a taste of home. While some of the other eateries looked interesting, she could always find her way back to the city later and examine them further. For now, nostalgia was far more appealing.

As she considered her options for her meal, she noticed that the tavern was filling with more and more patrons, many of whom were gathering near a small platform in the corner of the room. Shortly afterward, a minstrel came in to play. A young woman sat on a low wooden stool atop the platform, guitar in hand and a small bowl before her for tips. She began to strum, the music quiet at first but steadily growing to fill the room. When she began to sing, however, Keyt looked up in surprise. She'd never heard anyone play a multi-part harmony with only their voice and their instrument before. Had she not seen it herself, she would have doubted it had actually happened. Respect for the woman's talent growing the longer she played, Keyt tipped her a full sheckel once her set was over.

After eating her fill, she continued her exploration of the town. Eventually she came to what she sought: a shop dedicated to the sale of climbing and mountaineering equipment. She found a climbing set that came complete with the harness and pitons she would need for steep cliff faces. The quantity of pitons was decent, but she picked out another handful of them, just to be safe. Pitons, in her experience, were something of which it was always better to have extra on hand, particularly when heading into unknown terrain. She also got some clothing with thick fur lining that was designed for colder weather, thicker and more heavily insulated than even the standard wares back home, and then added gloves and boots with built-in spikes and a collapsible ladder for crossing the series of crevasses she knew lie ahead for her.

"Headed up to the mountains?"

"Yes," she replied simply as she pulled out her map. There were other items that she wasn't sure as to whether or not she would need, so she wanted another look at the area in which she would be climbing before making her decision.

"Crossing or climbing?"

"Excuse me?" She glanced up from the map to meet his eyes.

The shopkeeper gestured at her pile of items. "Those look like you're planning on climbing, so I was curious. Not many go exploring the mountains of late."

"There's something I need up there," she explained. "I'm looking for water from a specific spring that is supposed to be atop the mountains."

He nodded thoughtfully. "You must be in search of the waters of life."

She blinked at him in surprise. Apparently the lifespring was called something different in this empire. Or at least in this city. "Is that a common destination?" Nobody recently had known about what she had sought so she hadn't expected this shopkeeper to recognize the description.

"Of a sort. We occasionally have people come in here, inquiring as to what it would take to get to it. Most that head up the mountain come back pretty quickly; they're not as prepared for the climb as they think they are. When the going gets tough, they turn back around." He eyed her and her selection once more. "You look like you're pretty prepared for the climb, though."

She nodded. "I'm used to climbing the occasional mountain back home. Nothing as big as the Ram Mountains, but close enough for me to know what I'm getting into. You said most come back, does that mean the rest of them find the spring?"

"I'm sure it's possible that some of them do but my guess? The rest of 'em either continue down the other side of the mountain, or they're still up there somewhere. Can't really say for sure, but generally people who go up there just don't make it back to anywhere at all." He scanned her map, noting the spots she had marked where she had initially believed the spring to be located. "Looks like you've got the right area, at least, but it's not going to be found where you've marked."

"It's not?" Her brows furled. "Why is that?"

"You're on the right path, at least your ideas are sound. This seems like a likely place to find the spring, but it's nothing but natural water there. You need to track this spring here," he indicated one of the individual springs she had marked on the map, "back to its source." He trailed his finger across the parchment, following the waterway further up the mountain. "Here, this is what you're looking for." He tapped at a spot she hadn't previously considered.

She leaned in closer to see where he indicated. "You're sure about this?" Doubt was heavy in her words. The last thing she needed at that moment was to be led astray by someone telling her to go to the wrong place.

He nodded. "Most of the streams up here, they come from rivers and other small offshoots. A lot of 'em are under the snow cover, so they aren't shown very well on the maps. But this one? This one's different."

"How is it different?"

"Heat. This one's warm when it comes out of the ground."

"Warm?" she cocked her head in confusion. "How can water under ice be warm?"

"Can't answer that myself, of course, but seems to me that there must be something magical there for the water to come out hot from the ice, don't you think?"

She looked from the man and back to her map again. "You're sure about this?" She'd never even heard of warm water on a mountaintop before. As unlikely and fantastical as it sounded, she had to agree that it would definitely require magic to do something like that. Perhaps he wasn't leading her as far astray as she had worried. Unless, of course, the story about the water being hot was untrue. That was definitely a possibility.

"Sure as I am about my own name," he chuckled. "Though I've never been there myself." He stood and stretched, releasing a few small pops as he did so. "Bit too old to go climbing mountains anymore, even for a magic spring like this one."

She thanked him for the information, paid for her purchases, and rerolled her map. As she tucked it into its protective case, she asked, "Do you know where I might find a caravan heading up that direction? I noticed a pass nearby, so I assume it's used at least occasionally."

"I'd check at the south edge of town. There's always one caravan or another out that way, so if you're gonna find one headed over the pass, that's the most likely place."

Before heading out to find the caravan, she had one more stop to make. At the messenger office down the road, she went inside to send word home to her brother. She hadn't given Malec any updates on her progress and location since her arrival at Marisburgh and she didn't want him to worry, thinking that something bad had happened to her. She still hadn't told him what she was doing, not wanting to get his hopes up in case she was unsuccessful, but she at least wanted him to know she was okay.

That completed, she headed to the southern edge of town in search of a caravan. It didn't take long to find where the caravans congregated, as there was a large camping area just outside of town that appeared to be half full of travelers, wagons, and all manner of burdensome beasts. Torches illuminated the area, their light intensified by the assortment of cooking and other fires that were set near some of the wagon groupings. Bright flags and banners covered some of the wagons but most were bare cloth, just the meager necessities to cover the wagons and protect the goods they carried. She walked cautiously into the camp and began to make inquiries.

11

It didn't take very long to find merchants headed for the pass. About a third of the gathered people were either headed up into the mountains or had just returned from the same. The fourth person she spoke with about joining their caravan had an opening and was willing to take her along with his team.

"I'm only headed up to the top of the pass," she explained, "I don't need to go all the way to the next town."

"The top of the pass? Why would you want to go there?" He looked her over, as though trying to find any visible indicators of her sanity.

"I'm looking for something," she explained, "and believe to find it there."

"Your funeral," the caravan master shrugged, "but you still gotta pay full price."

"That's fine." She understood his position. Most people didn't truly understand the dangers involved in climbing mountains, which was the reason so many failed and died. Snow was lovely to look at, but it hid dangers beneath it, particularly when ice crusted the top. It was quite simple to view the mountain from a distance, decide to see what lay atop it and head up to climb, only discovering how truly cold and inhospitable it is upon arrival. It was the same reason the shopkeeper had mentioned so many went in search of the lifestream and turned back empty handed. The caravan master likely expected her to change her mind when they arrived at the pass and continue down the other side of the mountain to their next destination and wanted his coin up front.

Unlike the caravan with which she had traveled from Marisburgh to Leavett, this one was pulled not by horses but by massive hairy beasts, far larger than any animal Keyt had seen before. Each stood almost as tall as four reindeer, with thick hair growing down their bodies in curtains. Massive tusks sprouted from either side of their mouths, each of which grew down and then curved upwards. Between the tusks was a long snout-like appendage, which swung and moved about as the creature shifted position, like a tail growing from the wrong end of its body.

She paid her fare and settled into the promised seat, arranging her belongings under the bench to keep them out of the way. "If you have more than that," one of the coach hands offered, "we can store it up top with the rest of the crates and such."

"No, thank you. This is all I have with me." She appreciated the offer but had little that she needed additional storage for. She was not a merchant, nor was she moving to reside in a new area, necessitating that all of her belongings come with her. To travel lightly was a necessity, carrying nothing more with her than the absolute minimum she would require for the journey. Having anything more than that was just additional weight to slow her down. That danger was particularly true in a place such as the pass she now headed toward.

As the rest of the passengers and merchants took their places within the assortment of wagons, the first beast in line began trudging up the road toward the mountain, pulling its wagon behind it. Slowly, one by one, the rest of the beasts and their wagons began to move as well. Each stayed close to the one in front of it, maintaining the safety inherent in large groups. They didn't move quickly but they definitely moved with a steady pace. Keyt couldn't imagine much that would cause those beasts to slow, outside of an avalanche or other similar occurrence.

The ride up the mountainside was uneventful, for which Keyt was appreciative. No bandits or beasts accosted the caravan as they passed through the foothills, at least, none that she was made aware of. As with all caravans, a handful of guards accompanied them along the journey. Their sole purpose was to keep the ride as devoid of excitement as possible. As far as Keyt could tell, the guards were either entirely unnecessary or performed their duties superbly, likely the latter. Of course, the massive beasts pulling the wagons likely acted as an additional deterrent, as not many bandits would dare to challenge something so large and powerful.

The biting cold crept into the wagons as they rose higher and higher into the clouds, piercing through the passengers and causing them all to wrap their blankets tightly around themselves to stay as warm as possible. When the snow came, as everyone knew would inevitably happen, it came in sideways in tiny flakes, slowly growing in size and ferocity the higher they climbed. Conversations among the passengers, sporadic to begin with, ceased entirely as the entire landscape turned into a white mass, with few features to be seen. Even the trees, which had shouldered the snow at lower levels of the mountain, ceased to grow in the ever-thinning air. Walls of ice-sheeted snow rose up on either side of the passage, formed by countless caravans and other travelers keeping the pass itself clear. Soon the walls closed in around them, oppressive vertical sheets of frozen land that encapsulated them completely.

Nights were spent within the wagons, as none dared brave the frigid air for any longer than they had to. Even the guards switched out their positions with increasing frequency, taking turns warming up and thawing in the warmer covered areas, only to return to their frozen watch positions. The first handful of nights were spent moving, as the beasts continued to plod along as the passengers and merchants slept. When they reached higher altitudes and the ice grew thick enough to support their massive weight, they began drawing camp at sunset, circling the wagons for safety and building fires with wood they had brought with them for just such a purpose.

As the snows grew and the air cooled, Keyt felt more and more like home, a pang of nostalgia growing in her stomach. All of the places she had been to recently had been warm, far warmer than even what her homeland saw during the height of summer, so the cold air and white landscape was precisely what she needed at that moment. She breathed in deeply, savoring the bracing wind and sharpness of the air itself. The sleep she got when they stopped for the nights was deep and satisfying, the environment finally comfortable.

At the crest of the pass, when the caravan stopped to camp for the evening, she stayed one last night with the group, ensuring she got a restful night and had all of her equipment prepared and ready. The snow was deep, far deeper than even the snows to which she was used back home, with a thick layer of ice across the top. The ice kept anyone who stepped onto the snow from falling through but it also kept travelers from seeing any hazards that lie below, hidden from sight.

"You sure you wanna go?" The caravan master came to see her the next morning. "You paid full price, so there's no reason for you to die up here on this mountaintop. We can easily accommodate you the rest of the way to town."

"I appreciate that," she smiled at him, "but this is the reason I'm here. There's nothing for me in town."

"Stay safe out there, girl," he said as he began rounding everyone up to leave. "There won't be another caravan coming through here for at least the next two weeks, so I hope you find whatever it is that brought you to this frozen wilderness."

As she watched the caravan pull away, starting the ponderous trek down the other side of the mountain, Keyt stood in silence. "As do I," she whispered into the wind. Even the tracks left behind to show where the caravan had headed faded quickly, camouflaged beneath the continuously falling snow. When the last wagon disappeared below the hill, all signs of it vanishing as though it had never existed in the first place, she turned to head into the snowpack.

From such a high vantage point, she spent a moment simply appreciating the view. In the direction from which they had come, she could see the city of Sapphire, now much smaller and less impressive than it had been while she had been there. Beyond that lie the rich blue expanse of the Azul Sea, with the crescent shape of Sage's Island barely visible on the horizon. In the other direction, she spotted another small town at the base of the mountain, with the other side of the Azul Sea beyond. Until that moment, she hadn't been aware of just how far into the sea the mountains stretched. Beyond the waters, land rose yet again, quickly turning into a barren, pale brown wilderness with no life at all to be seen. "That must be the desert," she decided. "Good to know."

She marveled on how far she had traveled so far and considered how far she had left to go before she was done. The altitude caused her cough, the same cough most of the caravan team had developed along the journey, to worsen. The air was thinner this high above the ground, which made breathing even more difficult. Lack of air made her light-headed, a sensation she knew would pass once she got used to the height and thin air. While it was cold, it was nowhere near as cold as the winters back home, so she had no fear of frost sickness. This mountaintop, more than any place she had been to so far, felt the most like home.

"Just take it slow," she reminded herself as she climbed higher into the ice. "You're not in a hurry and rushing causes mistakes." She had seen far too many people make that particular error, rushing in too much of a hurry to remember safety. The last thing she wanted to do was to slip on the ice and cause a snowfall, or to trip and land in one of the treacherously deep crevasses. If that was to happen, even the spiked gloves and boots and the handful of pitons she carried in her pack would not be sufficient to pull herself back out... assuming she survived the fall in the first place.

The winds picked up, rushing past her and pushing her off-path a few times as she moved but she kept low to the ground to let the worst of it blow over her. The closer she got to a crevasse, the slower and more careful she became, not wanting to become a permanent part of the mountain. How many others, she wondered as she crept slowly along her way, had come this far only to fall victim to one of the mountain's tricks? Gods willing, she would not be counted among them.

The crevasses were every bit as much of a concern as she had originally believed they would be, as she was forced to cross a great many of them along her trek. The collapsible ladder she had purchased for just that reason came in useful each time, as she was able to find portions of each crevasse that were narrow enough for the ladder to stretch across and rest one end on each side. Crossing the deep valleys, she was careful to keep her eyes ahead and not look down, curiosity falling well behind fear. The sensation of knowing there was nothing beneath her feet was not a comfortable one, so each time she made it safely to the opposite side, she stopped to send up a prayer of thanks to both the gods and her mother, all of whom she was certain watched over her.

"Focus on the rungs, not on the drop," she reminded herself as she crossed yet another expanse of deep emptiness. "Focus on the rungs, not on the drop." Her foot slipped, not much but enough to cause her to drop fully onto her stomach, holding on to the ladder for dear life. The structure beneath her, the only thing keeping her from almost certain death, bounced and wiggled a bit as she landed and she sent up another hurried prayer. If one end of the ladder, or even one corner of one end was to slip, there would be nothing to catch her, no way for her to save herself. She would fall and disappear into the bowels of the mountain, likely never to be discovered. She would simply become nothing more than another person who went in search of the lifespring, never to be seen again, a warning for those who followed.

Despite all of her intentions to the contrary, she glanced downwards into the gaping blackness that awaited her. As her panicked breathing turned into another coughing fit, she clung desperately to the ladder, scuttling her way across even as she coughed, her vision becoming blurry from panic and light-headedness, towards the opposite side. When her hands finally hit hard-packed snow, she slid off the ladder, pulled it to safety alongside her, and rolled over onto her back on the frozen ground, eyes squeezed shut against the vision of the death she had only barely escaped, thankful to be alive.

When she finally had her breathing under control and no longer felt as though she was about to lose consciousness from fear, she opened her eyes once more. The snows had halted, one of the brief respites that occasionally appeared, so the sky above her head was a bright, pale blue. The color reassured her, the same sky that she had gazed upon for her entire life continued to watch over her now. She closed her eyes and sent another prayer of thanks.

One of the streams she had initially identified shouldn't be too much further ahead, so she pushed herself shakily to her feet and continued the trek. Her heart still racing and her body still trembling from the death-inviting experience, she struggled to maintain her balance with the first couple steps but soon relaxed upon reasonably solid ground and settled into her normal comfortable gait.

Soon, she found a waterway that she recognized from her map. It looked a bit different in person than it had on parchment but from its placement and direction, she recognized it to be the same one. "At least the map-makers were accurate," she said. Something struck her as curious, however. "How can the spring be so magical," she wondered, "if the waters manage to make it all the way down the mountain without any of its effects?" From what she could figure, the water should either still have its magical properties when it reached the base of the mountain, making her entire climb pointless, or there was some other reason why it was no longer magical further downslope. Deciding that she would never understand how magic worked, she shrugged and followed the water upstream towards its source.

Soon, she discovered an area that at first had appeared to be a very small, very localized snow flurry but as she grew closer, she discovered it to be not snow at all but instead found the area to be filled with steam. "That's strange," she mused to herself, her steps slowing in caution. "Why would there be steam coming from all the way up here?" With nothing but cold around, what could possibly be generating heat?

Remembering what the shopkeeper had told her about the lifespring coming from a magically heated source, she nodded to herself. Perhaps it was the enchanted water itself that caused the heat. Magic never made any sense to her anyway, as it seemed to follow entire sets of rules that conflicted directly with the rules for the rest of the world, so why should a magical spring suddenly follow rational behavior? She cautiously stepped into the fog-filled area, keeping a close eye on her footing. One thing she knew for certain is that steam often caused the ground to become slippery and this was definitely a place where she didn't want to lose her footing. Only a short distance upstream, she located the source, a pool of water almost as big across as the community longhouse back home was long. "This must be it," she breathed, choking on the heated air.

Something moved off to one side of the pool and she turned in alarm, almost losing her footing in the process. Had it not been for the spiked soles of her boots, she likely would have slid backwards down the hill she had just climbed. There, she spotted a handful of small, white-furred animals bathing in the heated water. She froze in place, uncertain as to what kind of threat these creatures might be and whether they would attack. When the odd creatures continued to bathe in peace, she sighed and relaxed. "I really hope that you guys are native creatures," she explained to the strange animals, "and not the people who came before me, seeking this spring."

The idea that these could be fellow seekers of the lifespring caused her to pause longer than she had intended to. Could this water, she wondered, be as cursed as her own family was? Instead of granting health as she had been told, did these waters transform normal people into these strange animals? Once again she wondered at the strange nature of magic and the quest she found herself on and found herself lacking in answers. "They've got to be natural animals," she decided finally.

She circled the pool, keeping a wary eye on the animals, until she found a small spot next to the group that appeared to be bubbling directly out of the icecap. Although the spring didn't appear to have any magical qualities, she realized that she probably wouldn't recognize them even if they were blaringly obvious. Shrugging, she collected some of the water directly from the source. "Maybe there's a surprise inside, after all." The animals, for their part, did nothing to stop her from gathering the water. Instead, they watched in fascination as she sealed the lid onto the collection jar. "I'm not taking much," she reassured them, not sure whether or not they could understand her, "and I'll be leaving again soon."

Exhausted from the journey so far and still feeling surprisingly light-headed from the altitude, she found a reasonably solid place to sit, far enough away from the pool so as to not get herself wet and to maintain a distance between herself and the bathing creatures. Although they had remained peaceful, she knew from experience that peace could become war in less time than a single beat of the heart.

"I hope you guys like music," she said as she pulled her flute from her pack. After another coughing fit, she lifted the instrument and played on it, letting the music wash over the mountain. She played the song of winter, which she felt was the most appropriate tune for the situation. The song had always made her think of the heart of winter, when the weather was coldest and the nights were longest, when summer felt like nothing more than a distant dream. Despite the desolation during the bleakness of winter, there was an underlying feeling of hope in the tune she played, of the promise that the snow would melt, the sun would rise, and the flowers would bloom once more.

As she played, a couple of the strange animals came closer, curious, to investigate. Appearing to be as hesitant about her as she was about them, none got close enough to touch but some moved more than close enough for her to get a better look at them. Their snowy fur wasn't completely white, as she had initially believed, but contained shades of brown and grey as well. They had appeared white because of the dusting of snow that clung to their fur. Their faces, which seemed almost comically human, were pink and devoid of fur. Whether this was due to the heat in the pool they obviously enjoyed so much or due to natural coloring, Keyt had no idea. They watched her as she played, eyes wide and clear as though they both understood and appreciated the meaning of the song.

As the last notes drifted into the mist-filled air, the animals slipped away once more. Deciding that was a good idea and that she had gotten enough rest, Keyt pushed herself to her feet and slipped the flute back into her pack, along with the jar of water she had collected. "I wonder if this needs to stay warm in order to work," she mused, "or whether it will stay warm on its own." There was no way to tell and she had no means by which to keep the water warm if that was the case anyway, so she shouldered her pack, checked the laces on her boots, and headed back out of the mist.

The view from the opposite side of the mountain from that which she had arrived was spectacular. Almost no clouds crossed the sky to obscure her view of the land far below. Even the most massive of towns and wide-spread forests seemed to be small from her vantage point, an appearance she knew to be deceptive. Just as how the mountain had appeared calm and serene, easy to ascend, from the ground far below, so too did the ground appear peaceful from her elevated height. She raised a hand to guard against the blindingly bright sun, made even brighter by the light reflecting off the snow that continued to surround her, she spotted the same brown, treeless area she had spotted previously when leaving the caravan. "My next destination is somewhere in the Fusite Desert," she decided. "I've never been to a desert. I wonder what it will be like."

Her next destination within view, she began the difficult climb down the mountain.

12

Snow was difficult to walk in. It was cold, it was slippery, and it had a habit of moving out from beneath one's feet while walking across it. If one didn't watch carefully to where they were going, they could fall into the ground and discover themselves in a cavern or stream hidden beneath the snow cover. That was the nature of the frozen lands from which Keyt had come and to which she was accustomed; it was the only life she had known until taking her current journey. That was the ground she whole-heartedly wished for as she trekked across one sand-filled dune after another. The desert was far too hot, far too dry, and just plain uncomfortable in every way she could imagine. Snow and ice melted once it made contact with a living body, a factor that some resented but Keyt loved. Sand, on the other hand, was remarkably persistent. The tiny blowing particles caught consistently in her throat and lungs, so she spent most of her time coughing as a result. Soon, the sand caused abrasions in her throat, abrasions which caused her to begin coughing up droplets of blood. "These abrasions will heal," she reminded herself yet again, "once I can get out of this infernal place."

Her destination was the Adlep Oasis, near the eastern edge of the desert. Durant, the first city she had encountered after her descent from the mountain, had been nestled in the foothills so she hadn't needed to travel far to find it. Thankfully, not only did it have a tavern with decent food and an attached inn with open beds, but Durant had also contained a transport gate. Despite her initial hesitation about the miniature portals, she had come to appreciate how many of them could be found and how much more quickly she could travel with them. After a meal, a wash, and some sleep, she had gone through the gate and found herself in Ankh-Ra, on the edge of the Fusite Desert. Ankh-Ra wasn't exactly near the Adlep Oasis but it was a lot closer than any other destination on the transport gate network and – more importantly - she hadn't been required to sail across the portion of the Azul Sea that she had spotted from the mountaintop, the expanse of water that lay between the Sapphire and Inland Empires.

Ankh-Ra had been filled with all manner of exciting sights and people, some dressed head to toe in gossamer clothing that was almost completely transparent and others dressed in white linen, clothing loose enough to allow movement but thick enough to keep the sand at bay. Keyt had looked around in awe once she arrived, marveling at how different everything was from what she had known back home. Here, just as back home, everything was white, but rather than snow causing the pale color, almost everything in Ankh-Ra was built from compressed sand, compacted into pale stone blocks that shimmered and gleamed in the blazing sun.

"Later," she shook herself back to her quest. "I can always come back and explore more later if I want." Much as she would have loved to spend the time looking at all of the wonders offered by the large town, there was no time to waste. "Malec is waiting."

She had already been gone longer than she had expected. What she had initially believed to have been a couple of months' worth of trip had already been more than double that and there was much distance left to travel before she could return. "Has he married yet?" she wondered. She hoped he had, that he hadn't waited for her return before furthering his relationship with Leoni. Moreso, she hoped that Malec hadn't put the girl off yet again, still fearing the worst despite Keyt's reassurances and his own knowledge that the Wasting would not and could not be passed to his children.

It had been in Ankh-Ra that she had purchased a camel, a strange beast somewhere between a horse and a reindeer but not particularly close enough to either of them for Keyt to feel comfortable atop it.

"It has no hooves," she pointed out, believing the barren feet to have been caused by some malady. "What happened to its hooves?"

"Camels don't have hooves," the stablemaster had pointed out. "Hooves are terrible in the sand, so these guys have feet that are more suitable to the desert than horses do." He stroked the rough fur on the side of the camel's flank as he explained.

Even stranger than its strange, hoof-less feet was the massive lump atop the camel's back, a hump she struggled to climb atop of in order to ride. Camels, she had decided almost immediately, were something she liked even less than the desert itself. However, there was no way for her to safely reach her destination and return to civilization again without one. Since the landscape was so parched, she had paid extra for a mount who knew the path to the oasis and back. She had come too far already to allow herself to fall to the unexpected pitfalls in the desert, a land about which she knew absolutely nothing.

"Camels," she swore softly, the third time in as many hours. "Strange word for such foul-tempered and odiferous animals." At least the blowing sand, which had worked its way into every available opening in her clothing, had clogged her nose so that she could no longer smell the foul beast. "This water had better be worth it." Just as she had done back home, talking to the reindeer when she had nobody else with whom to converse, she had quickly fallen back into the habit of speaking to her camel. The difference now was that she no longer cared whether the camel understood that it would make a lovely vat of glue. As a matter of fact, she hoped that the beast was aware both of that fact and her desire to facilitate such a transition.

Again, just as she had done since leaving home, she questioned the validity of the magical claims of the water she would find, if she found any at all. "If this oasis is so popular," she mused, "and well-known enough that even you know the way, how many others have you brought who sought this spring?" If the Adlep Oasis was such a destination for visitors, of which the trained camels were a strong indication, how could the waters there possibly have the effects she sought? "I'm on a fool's errand," she grumbled between raspy coughs. Her entire quest had begun to feel like a waste of time and she was tired of it already.

The only thing that kept her going was the faint hope that somehow one of the waters she had collected or would collect contained the basis for a cure that would save her brother and allow him to live a normal life with his new family.

Day after day, the dunes stretched endlessly in every direction. Had she been unable to see colors, she could have sworn that they were massive waves of water, rolling along the top of an endless yellow-brown sea. While she may not have been sick from the motion, the thought of being trapped in a massive sea of sand terrified her nonetheless and her lunch threatened to make a repeat appearance. She swallowed hard, grimacing against the sand in her throat, which only released another barrage of coughing. Gasping for air between bloody expulsions, she clung to the hated camel, the only thing keeping her alive in the arid wasteland.

The camel, for its part, continued to walk with absolutely no hurry along its known path. It didn't care that she was dying from the heat and sand. If it did care, she was certain, it was probably pleased. "How many others have you brought out here?" she asked. "How many of those have you brought back again?" Fitting that she would die here, she thought. At least the people of her town would be pleased. There was absolutely no way that anyone would accidentally stumble across her body if she fell from the camel. A camel which, she was positive, would just continue walking as though she had never been.

She lost track of days. Each day stretched out before and behind her, all around in every direction she could view, just as with the endless mounds of sand. Finally, the camel's unhurried pace increased, causing Keyt to look around in confusion. "Is there something out there?" Did the camel have some survival instincts that would indicate when a predator was around? She had seen the same thing plenty when her reindeer detected a wolf nearby, it was as though they sensed the beast before it even came into view. Was something similar happening with the camel?

Worse, she wondered what manner of beasts lived in the arid expanse of sand. How could anything survive out here, under the relentless sun and with no food, no water? She scanned the horizon, seeking any sign of the impending predator, but there was nothing to be found. All she could see was sand, sand, and more… "What is that?"

Along the horizon, just as the edge of her vision, the smooth-crested sand dunes turned jagged. As the camel brought her closer and closer, she realized that it was not the crest of a sand dune at all, but the very highest point of trees. Not the evergreen trees she knew from back home but the long-stalked and fern-fronded trees that had been present in Ankh-Ra. "Did we go in a full circle, you foul beast?" While she had clearly expressed her desire to return once her trip to the oasis was completed, that desire was contingent on getting to the oasis in the first place. The idea that she had spent so many days in sand-abraded misery just to return to her starting position galled her.

The camel, for its part, paid no heed to her increasing ire. Instead, it plodded along at its current pace, slightly faster than it had been traveling for most of the journey. Soon more of the distant trees came into view, allowing Keyt a better vision of what lie before them.

It was not the skyline of Ankh-Ra, as she had initially feared, but a small patch of life in the otherwise lifeless desert. A thick group of trees grew from the white sands, which indicated there was water somewhere within them. Keyt coughed and sighed in relief, hopeful that she could refill her canteen and wash away some of the sand.

The oasis was beautiful, she had to admit. White sands, even more pale than the sands that filled the rest of the Fusite Desert, surrounded blue-green water that glistened like a shining gem. She stopped at the edge of the pool and climbed down from the camel, thankful that the sands at the water's edge were more stable than those on the dunes. She considered the inviting water before her, wondering whether it was safe to drink. The warning about eternal life flashed through her mind once more and she hesitated. "Others have been here before me," she reminded herself. "Those people likely drank the water and none of them became eternal." As if to reinforce her statements, the camel stepped forward and began to slake its own thirst. That small movement was the last assurance she needed as to the safety of the water, as there was not a god she could think of who would want that horrid beast to live any longer than absolutely necessary.

As she cleaned herself, after having taken a deep drink of the fresh, cool water, a spray of water from the opposite edge of the lake startled her. Water erupted vertically, spurting high into the air for the briefest of moments before falling still once more. She stared in awe at the sight, continuing to watch as the fount ceased and the ripples on the surface faded into the shoreline.

"If anywhere was to hold magical water," she explained to the camel, which was busily drinking of the lake and paying absolutely no mind to the strange eruption, "that would be it." She climbed onto the shore to dry off, keeping an eye on the far end of the pool and waiting to see how often the geyser would appear.

The more she watched, the more certain she grew that the fountain was why she had been directed to this oasis. If anything in this desert was magical, it would be the eruptions of water. For the rest of that day and well into the next, she sat on the grass-ringed shoreline, trying to play her flute without much luck due to the constant coughing fits as her body tried to evacuate all of its collected sand and watching the small lake for activity. She measured the time between bursts, trying to come to a pattern, certain it had to have some sort of regularity to it but the pattern of eruptions eluded her. Finally, she decided that figuring out the schedule of the fountain would take too long. "I don't have time to sit here and wait," she explained. "I'll just have to go out to the geyser and wait for it to appear."

The camel, true to form, offered no helpful suggestions.

Not that she had expected anything less from the obstreperous beast.

13

Reeds, growing along the shoreline, could be just the thing to help her get the desired water. Keyt spent the better part of the afternoon gathering the surprisingly durable stems and lashing them together with an assortment of palm leaves and long grasses that grew nearby. It was slow and frustrating work, as the grasses broke as often as they tied, but slowly the desired shape began to take form. "It won't work for long," she explained to the camel as it settled itself into a shady area, folding its legs beneath its mass to watch, "but it doesn't have to. As long as it gets me there and back, that's all I need." She floated the contraption out onto the water to check its buoyancy, smiling to herself as she climbed aboard, pleased with the result.

Rather than fashioning makeshift paddles for the raft, she used her hands to guide the craft out toward the geyser, or at least reasonably close to where she believed it had been. "I probably should have paid closer attention to where this actually was," she muttered to herself as she gauged the distance between herself and the shoreline. "I think this is close enough." Now, all she needed to do was wait for the magic water to appear.

Appear it did, with a violent expulsion of force, which appeared without warning directly next to her. She shrieked and clung to the edge of her raft as it rocketed sideways, tilting at odd angles as she fought to maintain balance. The front end of the raft lifted and she counterbalanced, sliding her weight forward to stay afloat. Suddenly she found herself tumbling to the side, then she was clinging to the raft with the bulk of her body beneath it, the reeds and palm fronds looming overhead as the entire thing turned upside down.

Having relieved itself of its sole occupant, the raft thumped down in the water, barely missing

Keyt's head as she darted to the side in order to avoid the inevitable collision. Sputtering and wiping her face, she scowled at the useless raft, glowering at it as it bobbed in the water nearby, taunting her with its futility.

"At least I know how to swim." Countless days spent in the rivers of her homeland had taught her how to stay afloat under even the most severe of currents by regulating her breathing, lessons that served her well in the desert lake. The water, frothing from the spray, slowly calmed as she kicked her feet to stay upright. She considered trying to pull herself back aboard the raft, but in order to be close enough to collect the water she needed, she knew it would be pointless. At best, it would tip her directly back into the water again. Frustrated and growing angrier by the minute, she stayed in the water near where she had fallen, waiting for the geyser to reappear.

The water itself was clear and warm, much warmer than the bath water she regularly heated on the stove back home and far warmer than the springs in which she had learned to swim but nowhere near the super-heated temperature of the water on the mountain. Unlike the crystalline water to which she was used, the water in the oasis was tinged a slight green color, giving the sand at the bottom a strange and unnatural hue. There was no current, thankfully, so once the turbulence from the waterspout calmed, the lake was almost mirrorlike in its reflection. The small movements she made with her hands, keeping her in place near where the waterspout would reappear, did little to disturb the water's surface. She watched clouds drift by overhead, clearly reflective in the lake surface. Had she not been there for a specific purpose and had she not been unwillingly dumped into the lake, then perhaps she would have enjoyed the experience a bit more.

Two hours later, soggy and displeased with the entire venture, Keyt swam back to the edge of the lake and hauled herself out to dry. She was thoroughly worn out from treading water and wanted nothing more to do with the oasis, the desert, or the camel that had spent the entirety of her ordeal resting comfortably in the shade next to the lake. Panting in exhaustion and coughing water out of her lungs, she dropped onto the sandy shore and waited for the oppressive sun to dry her out. "At least the water isn't salty," she explained to the dismissive camel.

Once she was rested and relatively dry, she tucked the bottle of water she had collected from the geyser into her bag and approached the camel. "Okay, you obnoxious beast," she said, "You've had more than enough rest. It's time to get you back home." It took a little tugging on its reigns to get the creature moving but years of working with stubborn reindeer had given Keyt valuable experience on how to deal with stubborn, unwilling creatures and camels were no different in that regard. When it came to a battle of wills, there was little that could outfight a northerner. Slowly, with the same deliberately plodding gait that had brought her to the oasis, woman and camel headed back into the blistering, desolate Fusite Desert.

Her time in the water had done nothing to help her bleeding lungs. In fact, she suspected that the lengthy soak in the water had done almost as much damage as the sand through which they traveled, as she continued to cough up clots of blood the entire journey to civilization. The time she had spent in the oasis had done little to alleviate her disdain for the desert. If she had her way, she would never have to return to the horrid place again. Why anyone chose to live in such awful conditions was beyond her grasp. However, she had to admit that many made the same argument about the northern lands, so perhaps it was just a matter of perspective.

Her thoughts turned from the desert that surrounded her to the jar of hard-earned water she had just collected, which she considered with no small amount of suspicion. Not only was the Adlep Oasis a well-known and well-traveled location, her time spent in the water after her failed rafting experiment had done nothing whatsoever toward curing the abrasions in her throat. She had been almost directly in the path of the geyser when it erupted, twice, and if it held any healing properties, she would have expected to have seen them in herself. Even if bathing in the water wasn't enough to act as a restorative, the amount of water she had choked upon after her dunking should have done something more than make her cough and sputter for a period of time. Were any of the waters she had been collecting worth the effort of gathering them? Would any of them help to cure her brother of the Wasting? Doubts filled her mind, but she remained determined to complete her fool's quest, regardless of the result. To give in now was tantamount to an admission that she couldn't finish her journey, an admission she was not prepared to make easily. Fool's errand or not, she would complete the task she had undertaken.

Once they arrived back in Ankh-Ra, Keyt sold the camel once more, thankful to finally be rid of the stinking, ornery beast, and got an inn for the night. Before settling in, however, she headed to the tavern for a fresh, hot meal. The tavern-keeper, a girthy man in middle years, was busily wiping down a set of glasses with a dishtowel when she entered. Other than herself, there were few patrons in the tavern.

"Take a seat wherever you like, miss," the tavernkeeper set down his towel and the glass to greet her. "What can I get for you?"

"Ale please," she answered as she settled at a table. "And soup, if you've got it."

"No ale here, I'm afraid. How about wine? Local winery's got lots of flavors to choose from."

"How about beer?" She turned a hopeful eye toward the man but was quickly disappointed when he shook his head. "Okay, I guess I'll have wine then. What do you recommend?" Normally she wasn't much of a drinker of wines, preferring the heavier brews back home, but she was willing to take just about anything that didn't smell like camel. "Do you have anything similar to mead?"

"Absolutely. Do you like them sweeter or darker?"

"Darker, please." When she was handed one of the dainty glasses he had just been wiping down, now filled with a rich dark burgundy wine, she took an experimental sip. It was good, she had to admit. Not as good as mead or even ale would have been, but far better than she had expected. She finished the glass and signaled for a second. Perhaps there was one redeeming quality to the desert after all.

The meat in the thick soup she was served was not one with which she was familiar, but she took wretched glee in the idea that it may be camel. The more rational part of her mind realized that the odds of her being able to actually eat one of the horrid creatures were slight, but she decided to enjoy the fantasy regardless. Unfortunately, she knew that it was not the particular camel that had made her life miserable for the journey to and from the Adlep Oasis, as that camel was likely being pampered and prepared for the next unwitting visitor to the watering hole.

Thoughts of the oasis led her mind inevitably to the containers of water she had gathered so far. There had been three places that she had determined might hold the waters she sought, and she was currently in possession of two of them. She wondered whether one of those she had already collected was the one she needed for the curative, which would make yet another journey unnecessary. "Maybe I should just go directly to Dragon Keep," she mused to herself. She still had no idea where the recommended keep was, or why it was known as Dragon Keep, but it was the location of the alchemist she needed.

She scowled into her wineglass. "No, better to take the last trip," she sighed. She didn't want to waste the trip to see the alchemist on the off chance that neither of the waters she had collected was the correct one. If the alchemist she sought was indeed also trained as a death mage, she definitely didn't want to waste his time.

Now she just needed to figure out how to get to Ruschlack. Hopefully not by camel… or by boat, either. "There's got to be a portal, a gate, something to get there," she verbally hoped as she tore off a chunk of bread to dip into her soup, sopping up the broth, which was spicy enough to bring tears from her eyes. "I'll figure it out after I get some sleep."

That night, she slept fitfully, her sore and still-healing lungs and throat causing her to wake up at odd hours. What little recovery she had experienced from washing the abrading sand from her in the oasis had quickly been replaced by freshly torturous sand on the return journey. When the sun crested over the horizon, she gave up on further attempts to sleep. Instead, she headed down to the same tavern that she had dined in the night before in search of breakfast.

"Beautiful morning, innit?" The jovial tavern-keeper greeted her as soon as she walked inside.

"Lovely," she agreed out of habit, although from her perspective it was anything but. Her muscles ached from the trip across the desert and back and her stomach ached from coughing as much as she had been lately. She hoped that the last of the sand would clear out of her system relatively soon, as the less time she had to spend with this misery, the better.

"You'll be needing breakfast, then." It was less a question and more of a statement, as she barely had the chance to sit down before a bowl of porridge was placed before her. She accepted the bowl gratefully and began to eat.

When he came back to refill her water, when she was about halfway through the porridge, she thanked him and asked, "Is there a gate or a portal here in town?"

"You betcha," he answered with a smile, "there's no portal here, but there is a gate. If you're needing to travel locally, the gate's your best option."

"I see," she answered. "Where might I find the closest portal?" While she had a small sliver of hope that the gate system extended into the Dracott Empire, she knew that to be folly. There hadn't even been any transport gates in the Barberry Empire, which resided between the Dracott and Inland Empires.

He set down the water jug and looked thoughtful for a moment. "I'd say the easiest ones to get to are in Three Rivers, Hub, or Tradewinds. Those all have portals and they're on the gate network, so getting to any of 'em is as easy as gating there." He picked up the jug again and looked at her curiously. "Where are you trying to get to?"

"Ruschlack," she explained. "It's in the Dracott Empire."

He nodded slowly. "Your best bet is to use a portal to get to Tomens, I'd wager. From there, you can get to where you need to be."

She thanked him for his assistance and finished her meal. The helpful tavernkeeper had suggested precisely what she had already planned to do. Tomens, the capital city of the Dracott Empire, had a portal, so it would be easy enough to travel there without having to go by boat or, worse, a camel. From there, travel to Ruschlack should be a simple enough journey overland. That far north, the trip could be made by caravan or horse, even by foot if she absolutely had to. Then it would just be a matter of returning to the Inland Empire to meet the alchemist at Dragon Keep. Thankfully, what little she had learned about the keep included the information that it had a gate, so as soon as she was within the network once again, she could arrive there quickly and easily.

The three cities nearby that held both a portal and a gate were as unfamiliar to her as many of the places in the Inland Empire had been. Three Rivers was the first place the man had suggested, so she figured it was as good of a place as any to start. Still feeling terrible and thoroughly worn out from her ordeal in the desert, she finished her porridge, drank the last of the water in her glass, gathered her belongings and headed for the gate.

14

It took approximately ten minutes in Three Rivers for Keyt to change her mind. "This was most definitely not a good idea," she muttered to herself as she wandered through the packed streets, searching for the portal. Crowds of people in wizard's robes, many with colorful sashes around their necks as well, meandered up each street and down the next, their conversations all blending together in one loud buzzing sound that refused to subside. Many of the storefronts offered magical trinkets, which held no interest to Keyt as she passed. She had never had need of magical trinkets before and there was no point in investigating them now. If anything, they would just be more things to clutter up her pack and weigh her down.

Towering high overhead and casting shadow after shadow across the ground was a massive structure, a set of towers that stretched high into the clouds, joined together by massive bridges every ten or so stories that stretched across the sky. "That's the Academy," one person pointed out as she stopped to stare in equal parts wonder and fear. "It's where we all learn how to use our magic."

She had heard of magical training academies but had never been this close to one and thoroughly wished she hadn't been near one now. While Keyt didn't fear magic, as many of the people in her hometown did, she knew enough to not trust it. Those who had magical power often used their abilities to subjugate those around them and tales of magical warfare had filled her childhood. Stories of people who could fly through the air, stories of people who could read the memories in one's mind, even stories of those who could bring people back from the dead had enthralled her as a child but it hadn't been until she was older that she recognized these stories as not only true, but also as the warnings they had been meant to be. Magic, in almost all of its forms, was dangerous, its potential for abuse enormous.

And now, she was surrounded by it.

Had she known that the city was positively overrun with wizards and other assorted mages, she would have gone to one of the other two recommended locations instead.

Completely and thoroughly lost, she stopped in at the first store that seemed innocuous enough, one that displayed basket upon basket of freshly baked breads in its front windows and that smelled of yeasty dough. A small counter along the back wall held small sweetbreads, all of which appeared delectable. Even better, absolutely nothing she could see from her vantage point indicated that magic was in use in the small bakery. That didn't automatically mean that there wasn't some form of magic used in the baking, but Keyt couldn't fathom it harming the goods for sale at all.

"Can I help you with something, miss?" A positively tiny woman behind the counter smiled at her in greeting. "Muffins are fresh out of the oven. Care to try one?"

The offered muffins smelled as though they had been passed down directly from the gods so Keyt readily agreed. She tore a morsel from the offered sample, tasting it hesitantly. Her reticence disappeared instantly, as it was warm and flavorful, filled with roasted nuts, heady spices, and a fruit she didn't recognize. This was magic alright, just not the harmful kind. This was the kind of magic that soothed an aching soul and made life worth living.

"That's banana," the woman's smile widened as she explained. "Just got a shipment of 'em in the other day, so these are as fresh as they come."

She had never heard of a banana before, but she decided she liked it. After finishing the treat, she purchased a second one to enjoy later, along with a second muffin in a different flavor, and asked, "Can you tell me where to find the portal?"

"Sure enough, it's just over that little rise yonder." The woman pointed out through the front door and toward a small hill nearby. "Once you get to the top of that, you should see it pretty immediately."

Keyt thanked her, both for the baked goods and for the directions and headed out, feeling a slight amount better about her visit to Three Rivers. Once she crested the hill the baker had indicated, she found another reason to be pleased, as the line to use the portal was much shorter than she had anticipated. Everywhere else she had traveled, the portal lines had been thirty or more people long, but this line held only a few.

"On account of the gates," one of the travelers explained when Keyt asked. "Most people are only traveling to places the gates can take them to and gate travel is loads cheaper than taking a portal. You doing okay?"

The last question was in response to a coughing fit where Keyt spat out yet another clot of blood. "Yes, I'm alright. I just got back from a trip through the desert and I haven't quite gotten all of the sand out of my, well, everywhere."

The traveler nodded sagely. "Happens to a lot of folks when they go out there the first time. Hopefully you're feeling better soon."

Their conversation ended when the line moved forward, allowing both Keyt and her fellow traveler to enter the portal. While Keyt was headed to Tomens, the other person was headed for a different destination and moved to the opposite end of the platform. Thankful that not only was her journey almost over but that she didn't have to maintain a lengthy conversation, she closed her eyes against the disorientation she knew was to come and braced for arrival.

The dizziness and nausea faded swiftly, much faster than her recovery after a boat travel, and the air in Tomens was blessedly cool and slightly damp. While she could understand the appeal of living somewhere warmer than those to which she was used, the cool air soothed her on a level the warm air couldn't reach. She took a deep breath, coughed a few last times, scowling at the continued presence of blood, and looked around. This was her first trip to Tomens and she was determined to enjoy it.

No mounds of sand loomed on the horizon and not a single camel could be seen. The view was dominated by a massive castle, bright gray against the white sky, home to the newly-crowned empress. Everyone had heard about how Countess deMelville had inherited the Horn of Ascension from her father, who had been assassinated by none less than the infamous Dark Star. "I wonder what it would be like," Keyt mused to herself as she started along the cobbled road, "to live like that." Certainly someone so high-born as Countess deMelville, now Empress deMelville, would never know what it was like to travel the empires, to have to seek the means of maintaining her family's survival as Keyt had done and continued to do. "People like that have other people at their beck and call to do those kinds of things for them, after all."

Keyt wasn't jealous of the empress. While the people of the northern lands had a caste system, theirs was nowhere near as expansive or as oppressive as other empires seemed to have. In the Dracott Empire, people were born into a certain station and could expect to stay at or near that level for the entirety of their lives. Occasionally, people would wed for higher stations or be granted additional elevation due to other circumstances, but it was far different in the Barberry Empire. Back home, everyone was treated equally, regardless of which family they were born within. Only one's own actions and circumstances determined the esteem granted to a family or an individual. Those who sought the throne, no matter how lowly the circumstances of their birth may have been, had an equal right to challenge for it. Usually those ascensions, whether to the empire's throne or just to leadership of a specific town, were done by rote as the population recognized and respected those who were expected to rise as the previous leaders stepped down. Surprise challenges for position still happened, but they had grown somewhat rare.

As high ranking as the empress may have been, she likely knew no other life than that to which she had been born and had her own challenges to face, challenges that Keyt and others like her would never know. It was for that reason, the unknown life that was lived by nobility of other areas, which kept Keyt from feeling jealous of those stationed above her. Her position may have been low, but she held freedoms that few at the top could enjoy.

Thoughts of home reminded her that she hadn't maintained as much communication with those eager to hear from her as she had intended to. She stopped at a messenger-house to send word to Malec, partly to let him know that she was alright and partly to inform him that she would be returning shortly. After paying the message fee, she headed out in search of a horse, or perhaps even a reindeer. After her experience in the Fusite Desert, she could really use something familiar.

Despite the chill in the air, she was not far enough north to warrant the presence of reindeer, so she had to settle for a mild-tempered horse. Horses were much less expensive than the camel had been, so she was able to acquire one easily. She needed no stallion, young and eager to run. Nor did she need a workhorse, bred for carrying wagons and pulling ploughs across the fields. The one she decided on was a chestnut brown mare with black stockings above her hooves and eyes that had seen the roads leading to and from Tomens more times than Keyt wanted to imagine. "Come on, girl," she whispered as she stroked the mare's forehead in greeting, "I promise we'll take it nice and easy."

Ruschlack and the lake for which the town had been named were only a couple days' travel by horseback from Tomens. Keyt could easily have made the journey on foot, as it would have taken less than a week, but her muscles still hadn't recovered fully and she continued to ache everywhere. While walking could help to loosen up tight muscles, too much walking could aggravate things if she had actually damaged herself anywhere. The last thing she needed was to be stopped by injury after coming so far.

Although she had been mildly concerned about brigands, none had been seen along the roads between Tomens and Ruschlack. She spent most of the trip playing a few of her favorite tunes on the flute and chatting amicably with the mare. The mare, for her part, had little to say in return, for which Keyt was thankful. Mostly, she enjoyed the solitude. Much as she missed her brother, she was pleased for the quiet time by herself. "I'll have to find a nuptial gift when I return," she mused between songs. "Certainly they will have wed by now." Perhaps, she thought, there may even be a baby underway.

Her thoughts drifted back to the jars of water, safely nestled in her pack. Not for the first time and unlikely to be for the last, she considered what she would do if none of the waters worked as promised. "What if it was just a wives' tale, a fool's errand?" she wondered. "Or what if the actual spring was in one of the places I didn't travel to?" While she could entertain the idea of traveling to yet another place to get more water, repeating the journey she had already undergone, she knew that her quest had exhausted her and the chances that she would be able to do it all over again were slim, at best. And even that was contingent on finding the correct place to travel. Starting over from nothing was not something she looked forward to.

"But it's Malec," she reminded herself. "If that's what it will take to save him, I'll do this as many times as need be." She had made a promise to her mother that she would care for Malec, and it was a promise she intended to honor.

Even if it meant taking another boat or riding another camel.

15

Sometimes, it was just plain nice to be back in familiar territory. While Ruschlack wasn't actually part of Keyt's familiar space, it was similar enough to her own hometown that it brought forth feelings of nostalgia. She had expected to discover the town to be large, with a bustling metropolitan center and busy market quarter but what she found was quite the opposite. The town proper was only marginally larger than her own village, quiet and simple without too much noise or too many people. The only real hubbub was in the market area, which was about the same in Ruschlack as it was in every other town of equivalent size. Even though the weather in Ruschlack was warmer and wetter than that to which Keyt was used, it still felt close enough to home to make her feel at ease.

She arrived just before nightfall, so the sunset turned the lake after which the town had been named into a pool of beautiful colors. Pinks, blues, oranges, whites, and darker shadowy purples danced across the water. Nestled against the edge of the lake, the town was already in the process of shutting down for the night. Summer was in full retreat, the highest temperatures of the season nothing more than a quickly fading memory, replaced by lively autumn blooms that lined the streets in festive color. Even the trees were exchanging their green leaves for those of golden yellow, orange and red. As the shadows deepened, Keyt headed for the closest inn and tavern, hoping to get a fresh meal and a room for the night.

Stabling the horse was an easy decision. Since she didn't entirely know where in Ruschlack she needed to go in order to find the spring, the horse would remain a necessity. Thankfully, the cost for stabling for a night was much lower than the expense of selling it and purchasing a new horse entirely.

Exhausted as she was, still coughing out sand from her trip across the Fusite Desert and finding more of the same hidden away in everything she owned, she gratefully accepted the last available room at the inn, which was on the second floor above the tavern, and fell asleep as soon as her head made contact with the mattress. Noise from the bustling tavern below did nothing to halt her descent into dreams.

Her dreams, for their part, were comforting. She dreamt that she was back home in her family's long-house, her mother standing at the stove and cooking one of her evening meals. Soup bubbled in the pot and fresh crusty knots of bread with creamy butter waited on the table. The Wasting was nowhere in sight, as her mother looked as healthy as Keyt had ever seen her. Malec, appearing stronger and heartier than she had ever seen him in the waking world, was there as well, standing next to the table. Seated on a chair next to Malec was Leoni, holding a small baby boy who slept quietly in her arms. Warmth and comfort crashed over Keyt like waves as she surveyed the scene and she sighed in relief.

All was as it should be.

As she enjoyed the peaceful familiarity of her home, things began to seem strange. The fire, which had been flickering merrily only moments ago, turned into a simple flashing light, one that provided illumination but no warmth. The bread knots on the table turned to stone, impossible to eat. Her mother continued to stir the pot on the stove, but her movements became less fluid and more mechanical, as though she had become a clockwork version of herself. Leoni no longer held a baby; it had transformed from a sleeping infant into an empty bundle of white satin blankets. The peaceful smile on Malec's face turned to sorrow, tears ran freely down his face. Leoni and the bundle she held disappeared, silently fading from view. A cold wind blew in from outside, gusting around the lonely siblings and their clockwork mother, who continued to smile and stir.

Keyt woke up with a start, shooting to a seated position and coughing violently. Her heart was racing, her body coated in sweat despite the otherwise chilly air of the room. As she calmed, her breathing became easier and her pulse lowered to normal levels. While there were some dreams that happened regularly and some dreams that simply reflected on the things going on in her life, it had been a long time since she had experienced a nightmare such as that one.

Rather than trying to return to sleep, Keyt stood up and stretched. The sun had already crested the horizon, bright morning light flooding through the room. She rinsed the sweat away as best she could with the washbasin, wishing the basin was large enough to double as a bathtub, before getting dressed and heading downstairs. Thankfully she had gotten enough sleep to feel rested before being jolted awake, so there was no point in trying to continue. If she was awake anyway, she figured, she may as well get a start to the day.

"Mornin', miss," the tavernkeeper greeted her as she walked into the dining area. "Care for a spot of breakfast?"

"Yes, please, and good morning to you as well." She selected a table near the windows this time, both assured in the faith that the people of

Ruschlack wouldn't be as afraid of her as those back home were and to have a closer look at the town in the morning light. The tavern was near the center of town and she had a good view up and down the main street and the lake at the far end. It had rained overnight, darkening the streets and leaving pearls of light on the flowers growing in a box directly opposite the window from her. There were plenty of others starting their day as well, the streets weren't quite filled but could by no means be called empty. An assortment of wagons, each drawn by their own team of horses, carried goods from one end of the town to the other. A caravan had arrived at some point, evidenced by the throng of merchants who were already setting up temporary stalls at one end of the street. Other shopkeepers were still opening their stores, unlocking doors and sweeping walkways to invite passersby to enter and peruse their goods.

Shortly after she was seated, the same man who had greeted her came over with a plate of biscuits and sausage gravy, which he placed on the table in front of her. "Haven't seen you around before, now have I?"

"No, this is my first time here." Although she had grown used to not being avoided, she was still trying to get the hang of small talk. Discussions that had no point still seemed foreign and uncomfortable to her, but she did the best she could to talk without appearing rude.

"Visit'n people or just passin' through?"

"Actually," she turned her attention to the man more fully, "I'm here to find a set of caverns that are supposed to be near the lake out there. I don't suppose you know what caverns I'm talking about, do you?" With just a little bit of luck, this conversation may turn out to be more fruitful than anticipated.

The tavernkeeper guffawed, holding his belly as he laughed. "'Course I do, everyone around these here parts knows about 'em." Once he calmed down and caught his breath, he looked at her with serious eyes. "You sure you want to go there, though? That place is just packed full of dangers of all varieties."

"Yes, I'm sure. What kinds of dangers are there?"

"Well then, I suppose the worst of 'em wound be cave-ins. That place is underground, after all, so when the ceiling falls the whole thing falls." He looked through the window past her and examined the sky. "With the amount of rain we've had this season, I'd expect that the ground is still a bit unsteady out there. Might want to wait until it dries out a bit before you go cavin'."

That didn't surprise Keyt. Most subterranean caverns had the same type of danger involved in their exploration. As with everywhere, the wetter the ground, the less stable it became. She had actually expected to find less of this particular hazard, as the caves were supposed to be near the lake. Shouldn't the proximity to the lake mean that any areas at risk from the rain had already fallen from the lake? Perhaps she had been wrong in her assumption on how close to the lake the caverns she sought were. "Anything else I need to worry about?"

He looked thoughtful for a moment. "Spiders, I suppose. There are a bunch of Stillock spiders in that area. Every now and again we send people out to push 'em back away from town but they keep creepin' in regardless." He looked back at her and stroked his beard thoughtfully. "Might be some other critters down in there, too, but I'm not all that sure of what."

Despite his warning, she still intended to go see the caverns for herself. She hadn't gone through everything she had already survived just to be scared off by a few measly spiders. Pretty much every empire had spiders of some sort or another, so she didn't think that these would be too much more of a threat than the ones back home were.

When it became clear that his warnings had no effect on her, the tavernkeeper sighed and explained how to get to the caverns. "Entrance is just up the road," he explained. "Couple days by walking, less by horse."

She thanked him, both for the meal and the information, and returned to her breakfast. The dish was similar to what she often ate back home, which only added to the nostalgic feeling she had been experiencing since her arrival in the town.

She ate the warm, spicy meal slowly, savoring each bite. The gravy wasn't made with reindeer meat, but whatever it had come from was rich and spicy.

Once she was finished, she headed out to make preparations for the next, and hopefully last, portion of her journey. "That water had better be there," she mused to herself as she walked down the street. "At least, one of them had better be the right one." After everything she had already been through, the idea that the water she had gathered would provide no usefulness, that she had either gotten the wrong water to begin with or the rumors that had led her on her journey had been wrong, was almost enough to make her cry out loud. It wasn't the first time she had experienced such doubts and she seriously doubted it would be the last time. She simply couldn't be certain until she was able to confirm that at least one of the waters would work and the alchemist at Dragon Keep could do what she needed. Until that time, she just had to keep faith that she was moving closer to Malec's salvation and the end of the curse.

Her first stop was the general store, which wasn't all that dissimilar to general stores in almost every town she had been to thus far. Shelves of goods, both for those living in town and for those such as herself who were simply passing through, were piled high upon the shelves. Reams of cloth, bags and boxes and barrels of all sizes, spools of string, lanterns and a whole shelf filled with flasks of oil, cooking pots and pans, firestarters, shovels and pickaxes, the selection was almost endless. The wooden floor creaked loudly as she walked down the aisle, alerting the shopkeeper to her presence.

"Well howdya do, missy?" A tall, slender woman in a simple dress stepped forward, smile firmly plastered in place. Her hair was pulled back in a no-nonsense knot, tied and then retied upon itself to keep every strand under control.

"Hello, good morning."

"Help you find anything?"

"I need some climbing gear." While she still had most of the items she had purchased for her trek up the Ram Mountains, there were different supplies she would need for exploring a cave. Different environments often required different gear and she wasn't foolish enough to assume that what had worked on the mountain was sufficient to get her into and then back out of the cave.

"Mhmm. Got lots o' that here. Anything in particular?"

Keyt followed the woman to a rack of shelves at the far end of the store. A massive coil of rope took up the entire lower shelf of the rack, with harnesses, pitons, clawed hammers, and all of the other equipment one would need to scale a cliff or, in Keyt's case, to go spelunking. She didn't need the harness, as she still had one that was in good working order, but she could definitely use more pitons. Most of the ones she had previously bought were still embedded in the side of the mountain, likely already hidden beneath a deep layer of snow.

"If you need rope," the shopkeeper explained, "I can measure out however much you need so it can be as long as you like." That was unusual in her experience, as most shops simply carried lengths of rope already cut and coiled in predetermined segments. This was the first place she had been to where any length could be purchased. Not willing to complain about something that could be handy, she requested a far longer length of rope than she had initially intended to purchase. Too much rope simply didn't exist when it came to exploring an unknown area. Unless, of course, the weight of the rope caused more problems. That was about the only exception she could think of.

Before leaving, she added a small lantern and a few flasks of oil to her purchases. The oil was far more expensive in Ruschlack than it had been back home which initially gave her pause but as she considered it, it made more sense. Whaling was far more common in the northern lands of the Barberry Empire than it was in any of the neighboring empires, so the oil she purchased had likely been shipped from her own homeland.

"Where you headed with all this?" the shopkeeper asked as Keyt tucked the items into her pack.

"I'm headed to the caverns by the lake," she explained. "There's something in there I need to find."

The shopkeeper clucked her tongue in the universal sound of displeasure. "Do you know how dangerous that place is? So many people have gone in there and never made it back out again."

"I understand and I appreciate your concern.," she said as she cinched her pack closed. "But I have to go anyway." It was starting to sound as though the entire town feared the caverns. Just how dangerous was this place?

"Well, I hope you find whatever you're looking for."

As Keyt stepped quietly out onto the street, which had become much busier in the time she had been shopping, she said quietly, "So do I."

She spent a long moment looking up and down the road, examining all of the available storefronts to determine if there was anything she had overlooked or forgotten. Once she left town, she would be on her own once more and she didn't want to become trapped in the caves and unable to complete her quest because she didn't bring along everything she would need.

The scent of a bakery drew her attention. For a moment, she considered stopping in to see what they had, on the off chance that banana muffins had somehow become commonplace. She shook her head and dismissed the idea immediately. She didn't need any more baked goods, and if she truly wanted something sweet, she could get one upon her return. She was simply delaying the inevitable, some of the town's fear of the caverns and her own doubts creeping into her subconscious. She brushed it away and looked again in earnest at the shops, deliberately ignoring the bakery.

Finally satisfied that she was as prepared as she was going to be, she headed to the stables to fetch her horse.

16

The caverns themselves were located only a day's journey north of town, near the far side of the lake. It rained continuously along the ride, causing Keyt to be even more thankful than usual for the thick hide coat she wore. It had been tanned and cured to become almost entirely waterproof, keeping both herself and her possessions reasonably dry along the way. The horse, for its part, didn't seem to mind the rain at all, simply continuing to plod along the road in a slow but steady gait.

On the whole, Keyt didn't mind the rain as much as others may have. While she was concerned about the need to keep her supplies dry, she was used to cold, wet weather and at least the temperatures in this area were warmer than those usually found back home at this time of year. Additionally, she hoped that the rain would wash away the last remnants of Fusite sand that continued to cling tenaciously to her, despite her repeated attempts to wash it all away. No matter how many times she washed or shook out her clothing, she continued to find sand hidden within it.

Following the tavernkeeper's directions, she followed the road toward the lake, turning west when the road forked. Trees, present everywhere in the Dracott Empire that she had seen so far, grew close to the water's edge, making her wonder whether the entrance to the caverns might be hidden among the foliage. Enormous webs draped from the trees overhead like gossamer curtains and she marveled at their sheer size. "Are these from the spiders they warned me about?" she wondered. "How big are these things?" Familiar as she was with spiders and the webs that indicated their presence, she had never seen webbing as large or as expansive as this. "Or are there just that many of them?" She carefully examined the trees, looking for any signs of spider colonies, but saw nothing aside from the telltale webbing.

When they reached the cavern's entrance, she found a comfortable spot to hitch her horse, with plenty of lead to allow the mare to wander a bit and graze. "I'm not sure how long I'll be down there," she explained, "and I don't want you to have any problems while I'm gone."

She started a small fire in the cave's entrance where it was dry enough to ignite. For the last few hours, there had been no signs of spiders, webbed or otherwise, so she wasn't as concerned as she had previously been about the presence of the Stillock spiders the townspeople of Ruschlack had warned her to be on guard for. To settle her nerves, she spent a little bit of time playing her flute before settling down to sleep, hopeful that the comforting sound would help her to avoid a repeat of the previous night's dreams.

The caverns themselves were dark and creepy, even in the bright morning light. "Not that much different from any other cavern, I suppose," she said as she gathered up her supplies to head deeper inside. The night had passed without dreams, pleasant or otherwise, and she was eager to finish her quest and get back home to Malec.

The sooner she began her delve into the caverns, the sooner she could find what she sought and come back out again. Somewhere within these caves was the last of the waters she had spent so much time in search of, the waters that would bring an end to the torment that had plagued her family for countless generations. Nothing, not the dark or the threat of spiders, was going to keep her from finding it.

Water dripped, slowly but constantly, from the ceiling, as though the ceiling contained its own rain clouds. Keyt had to be careful as she continued deeper into the gloom not to be caught beneath one, the lantern in her hand only barely bright enough to make the tiny droplets visible as they fell. She swore loudly as one errant drop made its way between her clothing and the back of her neck, sliding down into her collar like a wayward garden slug. Her oath of surprise turned into yet another coughing fit. "Not quite as cold as the ice on the Ram Mountains," she decided once she caught her breath once more, "but not warmer by much either."

Not only was the meager light cast by her lamp largely ineffective at locating the random drops of water, but it also did little to illuminate the path, as the glow only reached a short distance away from the source. "Probably should have bought a better lamp," she muttered to herself as she turned away from the latest crevasse. "Bit too late to turn back and get one now."

Multiple times, she encountered crevasses, both deep and wide enough to completely obscure the opposite side and the bottom. These crevasses were not unlike those she had found atop the mountain range, both in size and in danger. The ones that were wide enough that she could not see the far side, she followed the edges carefully until it narrowed, or until she found a different path to take. The ladder she had carried with her since the beginning of her journey proved useful yet again, as she was able to use it to cross these gaps just as she had done high in the glacial mountains. At least in the caverns, she didn't have to worry about looking down into the gloom below as she crossed each expanse, as none of them were visible for more than a handful of feet.

She spent a full day wandering the maze of caverns, often discovering that she had criss-crossed her own path on multiple occasions. She leaned against the wall as another coughing fit overtook her, wishing that the air was a little less moisture-ridden so that she could catch a deep breath and finally clear out her lungs. Realizing that the wish was futile, she heaved a heavy sigh and continued deeper. Sounds echoed around her, some caused by her own footfalls and the occasional dislodged pebble but others caused by a source she couldn't identify. Multiple times, she stopped to listen but each time she did, the sounds ceased as well. It was almost as though whatever was causing the sounds knew she heard it and wanted to keep her from locating it.

On the third day of cavern exploration, thoroughly lost and unsure that she would be able to find her way back to the surface, admonishments of precisely such an occurrence from the Ruschlack citizens still echoing in her ears, Keyt finally found a small offshoot, barely more than a crack in the wall, that seemed to lead further underground. Unsure as to whether this was the correct route to take but not seeing any better options, she squeezed through the opening. What had initially appeared to be a hole wide enough for a person of her size to fit through with only a little bit of effort turned out to be much more difficult than she had initially realized, as the top of the opening closed entirely partway through, which meant that she needed to back out into the tunnel, drop to her knees, and crawl in order to make it through. It was a tight fit and she had to remove her pack, dragging it along behind her as she crawled.

Once she finally made it to the other side of the opening, between bouts of coughing and sneezing from dislodged dirt and gods knew what else, she could detect the faint sound of running water in the distance, sounds that had not been present before she had crawled through the tiny opening. "Finally," she sighed between coughs. "Almost there."

She followed the sound, pleased to have confirmation that she was on the right path. Time and time again, she had to squeeze through narrow passageways or crawl beneath massive boulders that blocked most of the path, until she finally reached on last massive crevasse. Just as the ones before, this one was wide and deep enough that her lantern's meager light couldn't reach the other side but unlike the others, this one had a stone pillar stretched across it that had the potential of being used as a makeshift bridge. The sound of running water was much louder in that area than it had been anywhere previously and she looked around, trying to determine whether the sound was coming from the opposite side of the ravine or from the invisible bottom.

"I suppose I'll find out one way or another," she said quietly into the silence. She stepped forward and put a tentative boot onto the stone bridge, hoping that it was as solid all the way across as it appeared from her current vantage point. When the first step felt would support her weight, she followed it with another and then another.

Fairly quickly, she was able to determine two things: first, the running water was coming from up ahead and second, the bridge grew a whole lot more slippery the further she went across it. Although the side closest to her had a few small patches of slick growth, they were tiny and easily avoided with just a little bit of careful maneuvering. She leaned down to examine the material, wondering if it was somehow different from the slick lichen back home, only to discover this growth was nothing like that to which she was accustomed. The fungus with which she was familiar grew in varying shades of green, from pale enough to be almost white to dark enough to approach black. But she had never before seen moss, or any other type of fungal growth, that was a vibrant orange to a bright red in color. Cautious, wondering what other effects this strange lichen may have, she trod carefully across it.

The further she got across the crevasse, the thicker and more numerous the patches became. They grew darker and closer together so that by the time she estimated she was about two-thirds of the way across the chasm, the makeshift bridge was entirely covered by a thickening sheet of treacherously slick blood-red lichen.

When she was almost to the opposite side, close enough to see the end of the bridge and solid cavern flooring beyond, she lost her footing as one of her boots slipped over the edge of the narrow stone bridge. She shrieked as her body slammed down onto the column, wrapping arms and legs around both sides of moss-coated surface, clinging for all she was worth and hoping she didn't lose even more of her grip to the slippery growth. A shooting pain shot up her left leg, not stopping until it reached her hip and she bit down against the need to change position. A small patch of red mold, dislodged by her motion, fluttered down into the darkness below, quickly disappearing from view. Her fingers searched for any openings in the lichen, prying through and under the mold and peeling more patches away, working on creating a clear area that would allow her to grab directly onto the stone rather than on the deceptive moss. Panting, her heart racing and her knees and palms scraped from the impact, not wanting to know what additional hazards that much contact with the slippery growth would have, she part scooted and part crawled the rest of the way across the ravine, keeping the bulk of her mass centered on the column and sliding herself forward, barely breathing until she was safe on the other side once more.

"I bet that's exactly what happened to all of the other people they warned me about," she said once she was on less treacherous ground, scowling at the dangerous bridge. "There's no telling how far down ravine that goes. Had I fallen, there's no way I'd be able to climb my way back up again." She winced as she stood, the pain in her injured leg searing again, this time far more than it had been previously. The rush of danger and excitement had dulled the pain, she supposed. As that faded, there was nothing left to dim the sensation now. She set down her pack and pulled up her pant leg, revealing a long gash down the side of her shin. There was no way to determine whether it had been contaminated by dirt or the red moss, not that it particularly mattered. The damage had already been done and any infection had likely already set in. "Great. Just great."

She sighed and dropped her pack to the ground once more, settling herself into a comfortable position next to it so that she could bandage her leg. It was bleeding a lot more than she would have liked, causing no small amount of concern that the injury was deeper than it had initially appeared. Just touching it sent waves of pain through her body, making cleaning the wound that much more agonizing of a process than it should have been. Once it was clean enough, or as clean as she could get it within the caverns, she wrapped the bandage tightly around it, hoping that it would not only slow the bleeding but also that the compression would help to ease some of the pain.

"I just need to hurry up and finish this," she said as she tugged the stained leather down over the bandages. "Once I'm back in town, I can get this cleaned up a lot better." While there was plenty of water in the cave, she wasn't sure how much she trusted it. Some of the water smelled swampy, as though it had been pooled there for some time. She had used some of her remaining drinking water to clean it so far, but she had little left and needed to ensure she had enough to make her way back out of the cave once more.

Limping and coughing, she followed the tunnel deeper and lower, circling around until she was thoroughly disoriented. Finally, she turned one last corner and discovered flowing water tumbling down the side of one wall. This water didn't appear heated as the previous water sources in the mountain or desert had, but it was the only one she had found that was running rather than stagnant. "Less of a stream," she mused, "and more of a waterfall. But this has got to be the right place." Relieved to finally have reached her goal, she settled her pack down once more and dug out the last vial to collect water into.

For a moment, she considered washing out her injury with more of the running water since it appeared far cleaner than all of the other waters she had seen in the caverns but immediately thought better of the idea. The warning about the water causing eternal life still settled in the back of her mind and that wasn't something she was interested in. While all of the legends said that the water needed to be consumed, or at least indicated if not outright stating as much, she wasn't sure what kind of effect would be had by bathing in it. The fact that she had been forced to swim out to the geyser in the Adlep Oasis wasn't lost on her but putting magical water onto an open wound had to have more of an effect than simply bathing in diluted water.

At least, she hoped that was the case.

After settling the precious vial of water carefully into her pack and ensuring that it would remain secure, and after rebandaging her still-bleeding leg, she turned to head back out the way she had come. Although she wasn't any more certain than she had previously been that any of the vials she had collected held the cure, or even the basis of a cure, for her family's curse, she was satisfied that she had done all that she could. Now she just needed to figure out how to cross the damnable ravine without falling and injuring herself worse than she already had.

She settled for scooting her way across, similarly to how she had maneuvered the final third on her first trip across. Once the red moss turned back to solid stone, she considered pushing herself to her feet but immediately thought better of the idea. Considering how badly she was limping only moments before, trying to cross while standing would likely just cause her to fall once more. It had been pure luck that kept her from tumbling over the edge last time, luck that she didn't particularly feel like pressing any further than absolutely necessary.

On the way back out of the cavern, Keyt had to stop and rest far more often than she would have liked, much more frequently than she had done on the way in. It seemed like every hour required at least ten minutes of rest. Much of a hurry as she was in to get back to town and then back home, the pain in her leg slowed her considerably, as did the cough that seemed unwilling to let her breathe. "Dank air," she grumbled as she crawled through one of the narrow passageways. "People weren't meant to breathe so much water. That's why we live above the sea instead of below it." At least, she hoped that it was just the moisture in the air that was aggravating her cough and not something more serious, such as spores or other effects from the red moss.

When she got back out to the first area she had been in, the area that she had gone back and forth across more times than she could remember, she stopped and evaluated each of the side passages as she reached them, trying to recall which led to dead ends, which circled back onto themselves, and which would lead her back to the opening, the breathable air and the horse to take her back to Ruschlack. Despite her earlier belief that she would be unable to retrace her steps in the maze-like caverns, she only made a few wrong decisions before finally backtracking her way to the entrance where the remnants of the fire she had set when she first arrived at the cavern still waited. She eyed the long-dead campfire thoughtfully. "One more night here would probably do me a world of good," she considered. "I know I need rest and some clear air would help too." Even as she considered the possibility, she shook her head and decided against it. The sooner she left, the sooner she would arrive at her next destination. "I can rest once I get there, and the air is just as clear on the road as it is here." Decided, she settled her supplies back onto her horse. "Probably even more so."

"Mother," she said as she looked up to the star-laden sky, hoping that her words could reach her somehow, "I know you've been watching over me, walking by my side through all of this. I hope that you're pleased with what I've done and that we've finally succeeded in achieving what you set out to do all those years ago." Regret twisted her insides slightly at her words. Had she set out on this quest long ago, before her mother had finally succumbed to the Wasting, perhaps Keyt could have saved more than just Malec. Had she known about the lifespring, had she gone in search of it while her mother was still alive, then she could have had many more years than just the scant few she had enjoyed.

But it was too late to think about could-haves and to regret things she had no control over. She hadn't known about the lifespring, hadn't gone in search of it, and it was far too late to save her mother. Malec, on the other hand, still waited her return.

Dizziness made her unsteady as she climbed aboard the patiently waiting mare. Time spent underground continued to disorient her and the loss of blood from the wound in her leg made her even more lightheaded than normal. She fought to remain conscious along the ride, not wanting to risk falling asleep and somehow ending up at the wrong place at the other end of the road.

At least, she realized, she didn't have to walk and the horse knew where it was going.

And it didn't smell as badly as the camel had.

17

Lights flickered as Keyt ran from pool of sunlight to tree-covered shade and back to sunlight once again. She darted around trees, bushes, and stomped through the occasional stream, not caring about how much noise she made or whether she was scaring any of the wildlife. In the distance, far off ahead, she could hear Malec's voice as he called to her, begging her to help him. His voice prompted her to run faster, to trounce the ground beneath her boots. Her brother needed her and she couldn't find him.

The sounds she made in her panicked run paled in comparison to the thunderous noises that kept pace behind her. No matter how fast she ran, the sounds always seemed to be only a pace or two from catching up completely. If her pace slowed, if she stopped fighting, if she took even a moment's break, it would all be over. She couldn't even take the time to look behind her, glance over her shoulder to see how much space she had, what the distance between them truly was. If she slowed in the slightest, the monstrous form chasing her would catch up in an instant and she didn't want to know what that would mean for her. Or for Malec.

She pushed bushes and low branches out of her way as she ran, scraping her hands and arms painfully as she did, but she paid the wounds no attention. They would heal, assuming she escaped. Everything would be okay as long as she was able to somehow get away. Darting around another of the endless trees, Malec's voice echoing in her ears, she risked a glance behind her to see whether the beast had grown any closer, to discover precisely how far away the creature was.

Oozing between trees and across the leaf-littered ground, the massive blue creature hunted its prey. Had it been still, it would have appeared nothing more impressive than a massive mound of watery gelatin that had turned an impossible shade of blue, the same color as the Azul Sea, almost three feet in height and twice as large at the base. It moved with impossible quickness, its body rippling and flickering in the dappled light. The meager path that Keyt had cut through the foliage as she ran was nothing compared to the wide swatch consumed beneath the wriggling blue mass.

As Keyt turned to face in the path she was running once more, she discovered that she had made a mistake. Rather than escaping through the solid floor of the forest, the trees suddenly disappeared, the bushes dotting the ground camouflaging the truth until it was too late for her to change direction. The ground fell away beneath her, Malec's voice calling to her again as she fell.

Beneath her, rather than the side of a hill as she had hoped, waited nothing at all. Deep blackness, the empty void of a yawning chasm swallowed her entirely, consuming her every bit as much as the blue mass chasing her had desired to do.

She woke with a start, eyes snapping open and breath catching in her throat. She flailed for a moment, certain that she had just impacted the ground at the base of the chasm into which she had stumbled, but she was no longer falling. Instead, her arms and legs landed on something surprisingly soft.

Bright sunlight filtered into the room through a set of cheerful yellow, orange, and white checked curtains. The bed Keyt slept in was covered with soft sheets and a thick yellow and blue quilted blanket. Next to the bed, a wooden chair held her traveling cloak and pack, her boots waiting patiently alongside. A low table near a door held a blue and white ceramic washbasin and a pristine white towel. Keyt blinked in confusion at the light, trying to remember how she had gotten there and where, for that matter, she was. The curtains didn't seem familiar, nor did the rest of the room. This was definitely not the room at the inn she had paid for the previous night.

"Ah, I see you are awake." A woman in her late thirties with close-cropped tightly curled hair peeked in through the door. She pushed the door open further and walked into the room. "How are you feeling, my dear?" Her voice was low and smooth, soothing in its own way.

"I'm alright," Keyt answered hesitantly. "Where am I?"

"You are at the temple of the storm gods Malaana and Oneid. I am the high priestess here, my name's Zanthia. You were brought here to me two days ago when the innkeeper was unable to wake you." She clucked her tongue. "He thought you were dead, but we knew better, now didn't we?"

"Two days?" She pushed herself up on her elbows, wincing slightly at the movement. Every muscle in her body was sore and protested loudly at the motion. "I've been here for two days?"

"That's right, and a right terrible mess you were when you'd arrived. Completely worn yourself out, that you had. It's a good thing the innkeeper called us to come get you instead of just leaving you where you were, else you'd likely not be here talking with me today."

Although the fear from the dream she had just experienced lingered, the details had already begun to fade. She remembered being chased by a strange watery creature and Malec calling for her, nothing more. "I'm still in Ruschlack though, right?"

"Right you are. Here we go." The priestess helped Keyt to a seated position and stabilized her by arranging the pillow behind her. "Comfortable?"

"I need to go." Keyt pulled the covers away from her legs and turned to climb out of the bed. "I appreciate all that you've done for me here, but I really need to be on the road by now." A wave of dizziness and nausea made her pause, stopping her from climbing out of the bed entirely.

Zanthia looked at her askance, head tilted in curiosity. "Now just what has you pushing yourself so hard, my dear? A day or two of rest can only help. Like I said, you were in a bad state when you came to us." She clucked her tongue. "You need to understand that you are not well, not well at all."

"No, really, I need to go. I will be alright; I have just been on a journey lately and haven't had much time to rest. I really appreciate everything you've done for me, but I truly need to be on my way soon."

The priestess looked less than convinced at her argument. "What has you in such a hurry? You were almost dead two days ago and now you're eager to run out the door? Surely you can spare a day for your own well-being."

"I really can't," Keyt explained. "My brother is in far worse state than I and if I don't return to him soon, all of this will have been for nothing." She explained about Malec and her quest to save him. "I'm almost done, but he doesn't have long. I need to go as quickly as I can."

Zanthia's eyes softened and she nodded understandingly. "I see. We will do just about anything for family, now won't we?" She helped Keyt out of bed and onto her feet. "In that case, at least let me give you breakfast and another bout of healing before you go."

"That I will accept," she sighed, relieved that the debate had ended so easily. "What do I owe you for taking care of me like this?"

"Nothing at all," Zanthia replied. "We don't charge for saving people, it's just what we do. If you feel the need to donate to our temple, however, we do have a collection box out front."

Four hours later, feeling much better after a hearty breakfast and a healing session by Zanthia, Keyt packed up her belongings, ensuring that the bottles of precious water were still safely secured in her pack, and headed out toward Tomens. The horse she had ridden on was still comfortably housed at the local stables, so once she paid the amount owed for the unexpected days of care they had tended to the animal, she was finally able to continue on her journey.

The cough she had been experiencing for the past few weeks had lessened considerably, due in no small part to the ministrations by Zanthia and the prayers she had received during her stay in the temple. She felt good enough, in fact, that she pulled out her mother's flute and played a tune along the way, both for the sheer joy of creating the beautiful sound and in thanks to both of the storm gods for watching over her. She had never been particularly pious to any deity in particular, but having ones so clearly helping her along her quest gave her courage. It only seemed right to give thanks to them for the aid they had given her.

The first thing she did after arriving in Tomens was to send word to Malec, letting him know that she was still all right and updating him on her progress. She could have kicked herself for not sending word to him while she had still been in Ruschlack, as he was certainly worried about her by now. She hadn't sent him any updates since heading for the caverns so there was no way for him to know whether or not she had survived that portion of her journey. In closing, she explained that there was only one stop remaining on her quest, meaning that that she will be returning home again soon. As she completed the message, she hoped it wasn't a lie. If one of the waters she had collected had the qualities she needed and if the alchemist was able to transform it into the elixir she needed, her words would remain true. Until those things were confirmed, all she could do was keep faith that things would work out in the end.

From Tomens, she took the massive golden portal back to the Inland Sea, arriving once more in Three Rivers. It was every bit as infested with mages as it had been the last time she had been there, so she wasted no time in making her way to the smaller transport gate. From what she had learned, Dragon Keep was close enough to Three Rivers to travel there by foot in less than a day but the time she had spent already weighed heavily on her and she was quickly running out of patience, recognizing that every delay only brought Malec closer to death. Even the possibility of gaining another delicious banana nut muffin while in Three Rivers didn't deter her. As she waited her turn in line to use the gate, a much shorter line than that to use the portal had been, she fought to keep her mind positive that she wasn't already too late and that the faith the merchants she had spoken with had held in the resident alchemist at Dragon Keep wasn't unfounded.

If this portion of her quest fell through, then all truly was for nothing.

18

Dragon Keep was not even close to as impressive a location as Keyt had been led to believe. She stood in the expansive, if not well-kept, courtyard of the keep and viewed her surroundings in dismay. A handful of travelers and merchants milled about, some appearing just as bewildered as she herself felt and others ignoring the les-than-impressive scenery and immediately heading along to be about their business. Hints of cobbles, stonework of a bygone era, appeared between the weeds and grasses that filled the courtyard. Most of the weeds near the gate had been worn down by the footfalls of travelers and an assortment of equally-worn pathways led to other areas of the keep. There were many buildings, just as many as she would have expected, but the vast majority of them were in crumbling ruins.

The only ones that appeared to be in reasonably good condition were the inn, the tavern, and a small storefront, each of which had a well-trod path leading to it. There was also a small building off to the side of the storefront offering tickets to the menagerie, which piqued her interest. Had she been less pressed for time, she likely would have gone over to see what that was about.

Nothing in the keep indicated that there was an alchemist of any repute available. As she looked around in growing confusion and concern, she finally settled on the tavern. If there was an alchemist in residence, or perhaps just nearby, the tavern would be the best place to glean information. The prospect of any kind of skilled alchemist working or residing within the keep withdrew with every moment. There was no place for him to work, no way anyone could do what Keyt needed in a place such as this. If there was an alchemist about, he probably lived and worked in a different location, somewhere nearby in the surrounding forest or perhaps down in Three Rivers with the rest of the mages and wizards. If the alchemist lived and worked in the nearby woods, Dragon Keep was likely just the most recognizable landmark to send travelers seeking his aid.

"You must be asking about Wendi," the young-looking man behind the bar answered her inquiry. "Yeah, she's probably around here some-where but she doesn't come up all that often. You might want to check with Phemie at the shop to see if she knows when she'll be back up from her lab."

His words, innocuous as they had been, stunned Keyt. There really was an alchemist working within this crumbling keep? Thoughts whirled through Keyt's mind as she walked back out of the tavern and across the courtyard to the shop. Of course the alchemist would have a lab, that completely made sense. How else could the resident alchemist create brews and concoctions? Keyt had somehow just not considered that it could be located underneath the keep.

Most of the people in the shop appeared to be customers, so Keyt didn't pay them much mind. Her eyes were instead drawn to a strange-looking woman covered in tattoos with matching sigils embroidered into her dress. The tattoos didn't strike Keyt as strange, as many of the men back home in the northern lands had similar markings etched into their skin, badges of honor for battles won or challenges overcome. The badges on this woman were far different from those the men collected, appearing more like words in a strange alphabet than images of triumph. What really struck her as unusual, which convinced her that this was no normal customer, was that the woman floated through the air on a stuffed chair. Her path decided, she strode forward with purpose. "I'm looking for Phemie, is she here?"

"If you're looking for Phemie, you've found her," the woman smiled pleasantly as she answered. "What can I help you with?"

"Well, I was told there was an alchemist here who might be able to help me. I asked at the tavern and they said to check in with you. Is he available?"

"He?" The woman chuckled. "She might be a little annoyed by that. Why do people always seem to think an alchemist has to be a man? No," she continued before Keyt could answer the question, "she's down in her lab right now with explicit instructions that she is not to be disturbed. Something about the experiment being a bit more reactive than she'd expected. Is there something perhaps I can help you with?"

"I am very sorry; I hadn't meant to assume she was a man." While she supposed it was possible that women could learn alchemy just as well as men could, Keyt had simply never seen it before. She really needed to adjust her thinking, it appeared, as there were a great many things that hadn't occurred to her before now but seemed commonplace among these people. "But no, I don't think there's anything you can help me with unless you happen to be an alchemist as well?" The odds of there being two alchemists within the keep seemed slight, but Keyt no longer felt like making assumptions about anything.

"Nope, just a witch here. Do you need one of her creations, perhaps? We have plenty of those for sale over here." She directed Keyt toward a shelf at the end of the counter where a wide assortment of strange items waited. They had been deliberately placed and angled to tempt shoppers, but she wasn't interested.

"What I need is something kind of specific. I think I have all of the ingredients to make it but I'm not entirely sure. I'm not even sure she'll be able to make what I need."

"Ah, I see. A custom order, then. Well, she's pretty open to making special things for people, particularly if there's something new she can learn about in the process. But she's likely to be a few days yet."

"A few days?" Keyt's heart sank at the words. "I hadn't expected it to be that long."

Phemie nodded. "When she's really involved in something, she tends to get completely absorbed in it. But that also means that when she starts working on your request, assuming she accepts the challenge, she will only be working on that. We have an inn you are more than welcome to stay in while you're waiting for her. I can send word to you as soon as Wendi surfaces again." Her words were comforting and reassuring, intended to calm the obviously agitated woman.

"I'd appreciate that, thank you so much." Trying to hide the disappointment, she turned and headed back out of the shop. Suddenly, her haste to get to the keep from Three Rivers and the expense of using the gate to travel seemed a waste. She could have saved a coin and walked with no loss. In fact, even had she made the trip by foot, she still would have needed to wait a while before the alchemist became available. Why had she not considered that there may be a delay in this portion of her quest as well?

After securing her room at the inn, which was much more comfortable inside than it had appeared from the outside, she settled into one of the chairs in the lounge area and scanned the keep, glass of mead from the tavern in hand. This was the first place she had been to which allowed ordering items from the tavern to be delivered to the inn, an idea she found interesting and had been excited to try. There was something very relaxing about sitting in a comfortable chair, away from the bustle in the tavern, and sipping at her drink in peace. The mead itself was rather good, not quite as good as the mead she could get back home but close enough for her to request a second glass once her first ran dry.

She watched with interest as travelers appeared through the gate, some on foot with only themselves and their group, others with wagons. Some of the wagons were laden with goods, obviously brought in the hopes of selling to the keep, others empty in the hopes of making purchases. The trading center at Dragon Keep was far busier and more productive than she had initially believed, yet another assumption about this strange place that she needed to let go of.

Exhaustion soon overtook her, as did another coughing fit that left her sore and breathless. Despite the ministrations of the priestess back in Ruschlack and her promise to rest as much as she could, the continued journey had undone much of the healing Keyt had received. The few days of rest she had experienced at the temple of the storm gods simply hadn't been enough to fully recover. "Well, I suppose I have enough time to rest now," she decided finally. She wasn't about to risk her time with the alchemist by leaving the keep until after she had at least spoken with the woman.

She spent the majority of the next few days asleep, venturing forth only when she needed food from the tavern or other similar necessities. The rest wasn't helping all that much, she believed, as the more sleep she got, the more tired and sore she became. The coughing fits were also becoming worse, often waking her up from her slumber. She soon lost track of how many days she had spent abed and how much time had passed since her arrival at Dragon Keep. Part of her worried that she had somehow missed her opportunity to meet with the alchemist, but she decided to hold faith in Phemie's promise to summon her when the time came.

A knock on her door roused her from what little sleep she'd been managing and she groaned out of the bed to see what was going on. She had paid for the whole week up front and didn't think she had been abed so long that her time had already expired. "Who is it?" She called through the closed door. A woman traveling on her own couldn't be too careful, after all, and opening the door to an unknown and unexpected visitor could only end in unwanted problems. Particularly in a place like this, with so many people coming and going. There was simply no way to keep track of who was there and what each of them intended with their journeys.

"Phemie says to come get you," a deep masculine voice answered. "She says you're expecting us to get you."

"Right, yes. Just a moment please." She stepped back over to the bed to put her boots on, stopping halfway through as another coughing fit tore through her. Once her boots were on and laced, she picked up the pack that still contained the bottles of precious water and stepped out the door, only to be greeted by the single most immense man she had ever encountered, not an easy feat for a person who lived her whole life among men whose average height was over six and a half feet. At second glance, he was even taller than she had originally thought, as he was stooped over and waited in a hunched position with his hands hanging down almost to his knees. Had he been standing upright, his head would have pushed through the high ceiling of the hallway. Keyt took a sharp intake of breath and it was only through sheer force of will that she stopped herself from retreating back into the safety of her room. "Phemie sent you?" Just what manner of beast was this man? Not anything she had ever seen, that was certain.

"Yep, that's me. She says to bring you down to the tavern." He turned to lead the way down the hallway. "Wendi's already there."

Still tired, sore everywhere and trying to catch her breath from both the cough and the shock from seeing her visitor, Keyt followed him down the hall and across the courtyard to meet the mysterious alchemist.

19

Keyt followed the strange man into the tavern and to a small table on the back wall, far away from most of the rest of the patrons. At first Keyt thought that she was being placed there in order to keep her away from other guests, similarly to how she was often treated back home, but she quickly discovered that the table she was directed to was not vacant. A woman waited there, seated at one end of the table with the hood of her cloak pulled up far enough to cover the majority of her face. All she could see of the woman as she approached was a wicked-looking scar running down the side of her face and onto her neckline. Just what had caused such a wound? Keyt wondered. And how had this woman survived it? The scar appeared deep, cutting deeply enough to kill an average person.

"I found your customer," Keyt's companion announced as they approached. "Okay if I have a bottle of the new wine now?"

"Yes, that's fine," the mysterious woman answered. "Go ahead and let Krun know I said it was okay. But only one bottle this time, thank you."

With neither another word nor a backwards glance, the enormous man shuffled off to fetch his reward.

"I understand you have been waiting to speak with me," the woman turned her attention to Keyt. "Please, join me. I am interested to hear what it is that you need."

"Thank you." Keyt tried not to stare at the strange woman as she accepted the offered seat. Not staring was a lot more difficult than it seemed, as the woman didn't lower her hood. Given that she had been told this woman was trained as both an alchemist and as a death mage, she wasn't sure whether that was a good thing or a bad one. "I have been told that you are the best person to speak with in regards to the lifespring."

"The waters of life?" The woman's head tilted curiously. "You seek eternal life? Why on earth would you want such a thing?"

"I don't. I have no intention of living forever. But I was told that if I was to gather samples of the lifespring, the waters of life, they could be used to make a curative for a curse that has plagued my family for generations."

"Hm. Normally I would refuse to work with such a substance but I must admit you have piqued my curiosity. Please, tell me more."

"As I said, I am looking for a curative for my brother. My family has been afflicted with a curse that leaves us dead at a young age; it took my mother not long ago and I fear my brother is soon to be taken by it as well. I heard stories that there was a way to make the curative out of the water of life, the lifespring, which is what brought me here."

"What kind of curse is it? The waters you seek may not be the best means of restoring you, depending on the source. Who cursed you?" Her voice was low and calm, steady as she spoke.

Of course the woman wouldn't fear curses, she was a death mage after all. She probably knew more about curses than anyone in Keyt's family ever had. "I have no idea who started it or why," Keyt admitted. "What I do know is that it is called the Wasting, that it is passed down along the family from mother to children, and our blood can cause infection in others even after we die." Her voice cracked as she continued. "That is why no one in my family can receive a proper burial, to be offered to our peace in the sky among the stars. We are resigned to an eternity under the ground where others cannot be harmed by our presence, where even the light from the stars cannot reach us."

"I have heard of this," Wendi nodded sympathetically. "There is a family afflicted so in the Barberry Empire that I heard a story about recently. You are from this family, yes?"

"Yes. My family has been in the northlands for many generations now. If you heard of the Wasting, it is likely that you have heard of us." She paused for a moment before adding, "my mother lasted a long time with this, but my brother has always been sickly so I fear he may perish before I find a way to save him."

"Phemie said you have some samples of water of the lifespring. May I see them?"

"Of course." She reached into her satchel and began withdrawing bottles. "There were quite a few places reported to be the water I was looking for, so I went to the three that seemed most likely and got the water from each of them."

"And where are these locations?"

"This one is from the caverns near Ruschlack Lake, out in the Dracott Empire. That's the last one I collected." She set the bottle on the table, centered in between them. "This one came from the Adlep Oasis. Terrible place, I must say. And this one," a third bottle joined the other two, "came from a spring atop the Ram Mountains. That was the first one I got."

"I am familiar with the water from the Adlep Oasis," Wendi said as she picked up each of the bottles and examined them more closely. "It is definitely magical, but it is not the lifespring, the waters of life you referred to."

"Oh." Try as she might, Keyt couldn't keep the disappointment from her voice. Despite the fact that she had suspected as much herself, she had still held out hope that her terrible journey across the Fusite Desert hadn't been in vain. Once again, she had been wrong.

"Don't be mistaken, as I said the water you collected is magical. In fact, I have a sample similar to this in my lab. I am quite familiar with all of its properties, none of which involve healing."

"What about the other two?"

"Now, those are interesting. I haven't worked with either of these, although I have heard rumors similar to those you yourself said you had heard. I can work with these and see what kind of qualities each of the samples has. If either is useful for your purposes, we will know soon enough."

Hope, almost forgotten since the early days of her journey, began to glow in her chest. "How long do you expect that to take?" Could this all really work? Was this woman actually able to make the potion to cure her brother after all?

"That depends entirely on what I find. If there are no magical properties, the answer will be quick. If there are properties to analyze, that can take a bit longer. I would expect up to a week, assuming that both of these have some type of properties to them."

Keyt's heart sank yet again. She had hoped the process would be much swifter, as each day that passed brought her brother that much closer to death and his wife Leoni that much closer to becoming a widow. But if that was how long the alchemist would need to do what she needed to, there was little Keyt could argue on it. A week was nothing compared to the amount of time she had already spent on her quest. Much as she would have loved a quick solution, nothing worth having came easily, as she well understood already. "I suppose that will have to do," she said finally. "Will you let me know as soon as you've discovered something?"

"Absolutely. You will be the first to know." She smiled and added, "aside from me, of course."

After their conversation concluded, Keyt headed back to the tavern to pay for another week. There was nowhere within the keep for her to send word to Malec about the delay, so she hoped that he understood that she was going as fast as she could and that she would be home as soon as possible. For a moment, she considered heading down to Three Rivers to find a messenger but decided against it. Much as she wanted to keep her brother informed, she much more wanted to stay near Dragon Keep in case the mysterious alchemist uncovered something important. It simply wouldn't do for her to delay the process any further just because of a simple run to town for a message. Even if that trip also held the prospect of a banana muffin.

One evening, after she had finished the night's meal, she went outside to a grassy, flower-covered area of the keep that appeared largely unused. She had discovered the spot a few days previously and appreciated the solitude. It also gave her a comfortable place to sit and think while playing a tune on her flute to keep her spirits up. She hadn't been there long before she felt a presence approaching. Wary but not scared, she stopped playing, lowered her flute and turned to face the newcomer.

"Please, don't stop on my account," Phemie laughed as she stepped lightly from the air to the ground. "You play beautifully. I've been hearing what sounded like music for the last few nights but hadn't been able to uncover the source quite yet, so I'm glad to have found you this time."

Keyt looked from the witch to the instrument in her hand. "My apologies. I hadn't meant to disturb anyone."

"Not at all. I was quite enjoying the music and wanted to know to whom I should express my appreciation." Her eyes lowered to the flute still in Keyt's hands. "That instrument of yours looks well-loved indeed. May I have a closer look?"

Keyt blinked in surprise and handed it over. "It was my mother's," she explained. "I'm not nearly as good with it as she was."

"I imagine that playing it as you have been lets you feel closer to your mother," Phemie said in a soft voice as she finished her examination and handed the instrument back. "How long ago did you lose her?"

"Less than a year." Keyt tucked the flute back into its protective pouch. "It was only a few days before she passed that she gave it to me so that it would stay in the family."

"I'm sure she is pleased that you have been using it. A wonderful heirloom such as that deserves so much more than just being placed on a shelf and forgotten."

"May I ask a question or two of you?"

"Of course, I am at your disposal. What would you like to know?"

"About Wendi, your alchemist. Is she truly as good as everyone seems to believe she is?"

Phemie chuckled at the question. "Well, first of all, she's not my alchemist. I guess you could say it's more like I am her witch. She owns this keep and everything in it. So she is mistress here, not I."

"Oh! I hadn't realized. I am so sorry for the assumption."

"No need to apologize. It's a pretty common misunderstanding since she doesn't come out to meet the people who come to visit very often. Most assume that because I am the one they see,

I am the one in charge of everything." Her face sobered. "But in response to your question, yes. She is quite talented indeed. If you're worried about whether or not she will be able to make the item you have requested of her, you have nothing to fear. Even if the ingredients you brought for her aren't quite what she needs, she will find a way to deliver what you asked for. That's just how she is. Once she gets her hands on an idea, particularly a challenging one, there's not much stopping her."

"I see. That is quite the relief." Her worries about not having found the correct water after all abated somewhat, she asked, "why does she wear that hood over her face? It does make it difficult to speak with her."

Phemie nodded again. "She knows. But her eyes are rather, well, strange, so she wears the cloak with the hood up to keep others from being unnerved by her appearance."

"Strange how?" Images of scars, similar to the one visible down the side of Wendi's face, shuddered through her mind. Just how much of her face did the scars cover, she wondered.

"That is not for me to divulge. If she decides to show you, that is her decision to make. But there is nothing for you to fear from her, or from anyone else here for that matter." The witch stood to leave. I really must return to my work, otherwise who knows what kind of mess Crucian and Jaeger will get themselves into." Effortlessly, she lifted into the air, gliding rather than walking as she headed back toward the main area of the keep.

"Oh! One other thing." Phemie turned back to face Keyt. "If you are interested, and please do not feel pressured in any way, we would love to have you play at the tavern at some point during your stay here. I'm sure others would enjoy hearing your music as much as I have been."

Surprised and taken slightly aback by the invitation, Keyt nodded. "I would be happy to." She'd never played in front of a crowd before, large or small, so she hoped she wouldn't turn out to be a disappointment. But the people of Dragon Keep had been so kind to her, she wouldn't have felt right turning down the invitation.

20

Keyt spent just over a week at Dragon Keep after her meeting with Wendi, waiting anxiously for news from the alchemist and playing for the crowds in the tavern each night. Although the offer from Phemie had initially been for a night or two of playing, the experience had been an enjoyable one for Keyt, enough so that when Phemie mentioned being interested in more performances, Keyt had agreed immediately. She still didn't believe that she was skilled enough to even ask for tips in return for her playing but a bowl to collect coins appeared every time she played regardless and there were always a small handful of coins within it at the end of her time on stage.

She still spent the majority of her time while waiting for word to come from Wendi abed, trying to rest and relax as much as possible. The rooms were surprisingly comfortable, clean and in decent repair, particularly when compared to the rest of the keep. On her third day of waiting, Crucian, the same strange man who had fetched her for her meeting with Wendi, came to her room again. When the knock came, Keyt had been overjoyed, thinking that the curative had already been completed, far ahead of schedule, but her hopes were dashed upon realizing that was not the case.

"Phemie sent this for you," he said, holding out a bottle. "She says you need to rest your lungs or something like that and this will help you feel a lot better." He thrust the bottle into her hands as he spoke.

"Thank you," she accepted the bottle and eyed it curiously. "I hadn't meant to disturb anyone."

"Just drink it," he said as he turned to leave. "Tastes bad but feels good."

Tastes bad was about as much of an understatement as he could have made, Keyt realized as she took a swig of the offered medicine. While most medications didn't taste good, they were usually at least made palatable with herbs and sweeteners added to offset the natural flavor. While this concoction held the same, it did little to ease its consumption. She gagged trying it the first time and had to sit on her bed, trying to not upheave everything she had just swallowed. "This is worse than being on a boat," she decided. "It tastes like licorice root mixed with mint leaves and some sort of honey, but with such a bitterness it's as though the throat refuses to accept it."

Once the nausea from swallowing the medication subsided, Keyt had to admit that it seemed to help ease her coughing. It didn't stop it completely but she was able to take a full, deep breath for the first time in days. Even more, the ache in her chest eased, the pain subsiding quickly. "Worth it," she agreed. "Tastes bad but feels good. He was right."

Heeding the witch's advice to rest her lungs as much as possible, she tried to not exert herself overly much while she waited. When she wasn't sleeping, she wandered around the keep's grounds, exploring and watching what was going on around her. There seemed to be a lot of people traveling to and from the keep, many more than she had initially expected. The majority of the visitors arrived and departed through the same gate Keyt herself had used, not surprising considering the dangers of the roads in the Inland Empire. Most notorious were the pirates, which many of the travelers were happy to explain their own adventures and encounters with the dangerous brigands of the seas. The Pirate Run, a river notorious for the quantity of pirates who patrolled its length, was close by as well. Keyt had heard mention of the Pirate Run once, long ago, but had all but forgotten about it during her journey.

"They've been acting up a lot more lately," one of the merchants explained. "We lost a whole ship to 'em not too long ago."

"Not many of the shipping companies are safe lately," another agreed. "Unless they got really good guardians, and I mean really good, nobody's safe."

"I hear even McClannahan's been having trouble with 'em lately."

"Yep. They lost one of their guardians a while ago, one of the new ones, after her weapons got broken. She's been off getting new ones made for some time now."

"It's not just here in the Inland Sea, either. They've been moving north into Barberry too."

Keyt's ears pricked up at the mention of her home empire. She knew that pirates were dangerous and that they had been spotted in the Barberry Empire somewhat recently but there had been little news about their activities since she had left so she listened with interest. Had they really increased their activity since she'd been gone? And how were her people handling their presence in the northern lands?

"Sounds like they're trying to get a foothold across the entire coastline of the Azul Sea."

"The whole coastline?" the first one guffawed. "That would take an army. More than one, I reckon. No way those pirates are strong enough to take the whole seaboard."

"I'm telling you, they're expanding all right. And if they're not taking over the whole coastline, then they're up to something else."

Conversation changed after that exchange so after listening for only another moment or two, long enough to determine that there was little in the new topic to hold her interest, Keyt stopped eavesdropping. Not that there had been much useful information in the conversation up to that point but not hearing anything good was a bit disappointing. Curious as she was about the increased pirates in the Barberry Empire, she wasn't overly concerned. After all, if there was one thing her people were good at, it was driving away invaders. The landscape itself helped much with that, as very few were as adapted to the cold north as the locals were.

Long days were spent waiting after her initial meeting with Wendi, each day filled with hopes that it would be the day for her to receive word that the curative she needed was ready, each day culminating in the disappointment of realizing she had to wait another day for such a blessing. Early in the afternoon of the ninth day, Crucian again came to see her. At first Keyt thought he was bringing her another bottle of Phemie's elixir, as he always seemed to deliver a fresh one when Keyt was about to run out. This time, however, he carried no bottle. Instead, he explained that he had been instructed to bring her to the tavern for another meeting.

"I wanted to give you an update," the alchemist explained as Keyt took her seat across from her. "I'm not completely done yet but I am making progress and the results I'm getting so far are promising. One of the samples you gave me does appear to have the properties you're looking for, so I have started focusing on that one and refining it."

Despite Phemie's assurances that Wendi would be able to create what she had asked for, Keyt's faith in such had been starting to waver over the last few days. When the first week had gone by with no word on Wendi's experimentation, doubts had crept in. Those doubts had quickly grown into discouragement that she would be able to complete her quest in time to save her brother. Now, all trace of discouragement and doubt disappeared with just a few short words from the cloaked woman before her. "How much longer?" She couldn't hide the eagerness from her voice as she spoke, leaning closer in anticipation. "How long do you expect this to take?"

"Not much," Wendi reassured her. "I still need a little more time to ensure that I have the formulas correct and to do a little more testing. The last thing we want is to give this to you and have it cause some unexpected problems that need to be tended to as well. I will let you know as soon as I have it ready, likely another three days."

Three days. After all of the time she had already spent, all of the traveling across four empires, Keyt could hardly believe that the goal of her quest would be available in only three short days. She stayed at the table, blinking in stunned silence, as Wendi excused herself and headed back to her laboratory. Almost immediately, a glass of brandy appeared on the table before her.

"On the house," Phemie explained as she settled herself into Wendi's vacated seat. "You looked like you could use it."

"She said three days," Keyt whispered. "It's almost here."

"Didn't I tell you?" Phemie reached across the table to pat Keyt's hand reassuringly. "You have nothing to worry about. Whatever it takes, she'll make it for you."

"My mother," Keyt choked out, her voice barely audible under the din in the bustling tavern, "spent her whole life looking for this and never even came close. She died believing that there was no cure out there, that we were doomed to suffer for an eternity or until the bloodline ended." Tears threatened, clouding her vision and fogging up the table before her and the woman who sat across.

"And now you have succeeded." The witch smiled again. "She would be so proud of you for everything you've done."

"Why didn't I do this sooner?" The threatening tears overflowed, coursing down her cheeks as she realized the cure was at hand. "I could have saved her too." She reached up to wipe away the moisture, a futile effort as more replaced it as soon as she moved her hand away.

"If I had to hazard a guess, you stayed by your mother so that she would have people she loved around her. If I was in her position, I would be happy to know that you were there with her, that you were safe at that moment, rather than running around as you have been to leave her alone."

Keyt nodded and finally reached for the glass of brandy. Her hands shook with emotion, so she used both of them to steady the fragile glass.

"There's no sense in beating yourself up over what you could have done. Things happen when they are supposed to happen, that's how life works. If your mother was meant to have been cured, she would have found the same information you found. All of this is happening the way it is supposed to. Just be glad that you are able to do this now."

Apparently sensing that Keyt needed to be left alone with her thoughts, Phemie retreated after that brief exchange.

Three days later, just as she had promised, Wendi sent for Keyt again. This time, when Keyt arrived, there was a vial resting in the center of the table. Keyt's name was written in clear, legible print in black ink on the side of the vial. "Is that what I think it is?"

"Yes. But you need to understand there is only one dose here. The water you collected only allowed me to make a single dose." She slid the vial across the table toward her. "Given your pressing need for this, I figured that giving this to you now would be far more important to you than waiting for me to go get more water to make additional doses."

"It's fine. More than fine. One dose was all I need. All I ever needed." She picked up the vial and looked closely at it. There was no visible difference between the water in the vial and the water she had brought with her, but it didn't matter. As long as it did the job, that was all she needed. "How much do I owe you for this?" Any price at all was acceptable. Her brother's life was worth any amount the woman could quote.

"Nothing at all." When Keyt looked up at her in shock, certain that she hadn't heard correctly, she explained. "Knowing where the water you brought to me came from is more than enough compensation. That means that I can go and get more any time I need to."

Curiosity compelled her to ask. "Which one was it?"

Wendi shook her head, a faint smile playing at the corners of her mouth. "That is my secret now, part of the payment. To ensure others cannot go out and recreate what I have done before I finish my own experiments with it."

"I can't thank you enough for this," Keyt stood and clutched the vial to her chest. "I, my entire family, will ever be grateful for all that you have done for me. For us. For all that all of you here at Dragon Keep have done."

Wendi's mouth stopped playing at a smile and curled up in a real one. "Go. I'm sure your brother is anxiously waiting for you."

"Yes. Thank you." Needing no further encouragement, she turned and headed to her room at the inn. She didn't have many belongings to pack, as she had kept everything as ready to go as possible. Only a few remaining items needed to be packed away before she was ready to go. To return home, to her brother, where she belonged. To finish her quest, the journey she had taken what felt like a lifetime ago, to save her brother.

Fifteen minutes later, she stepped through the transport gate. The gate network, she discovered with immense pleasure, had expanded in her absence, so she was able to travel almost all the way home via the gate without having to board another horrid boat. She purchased a reindeer at the first available seller, eager to make the last and final leg of her journey as swiftly as possible. "I'm coming home, Malec," she explained into the air as she trotted down the road.

"Hold on just a little bit longer for me, I'm coming home!"

21

The sun rose, sending waves of pink and orange shimmering across the horizon in sharp contrast to the heavy black clouds that loomed overhead. Thick puffs of snow fell, earlier in the season than usual for snowfall but not so early as to be shocking. At the base of a low hill, a scant handful of people gathered. Most notable of these were a tiny woman whose clothes and body were covered in sigils and a taller, cloak-enshrouded woman, both of whom stood in respectful silence. All of the others gathered kept their distance from the mysterious pair, uncertain as to their presence and what it meant.

Slowly, more people arrived, including a curly-haired woman bearing the robes that indicated she was a high priestess of the storm gods. Her presence in town was odd indeed, as the storm gods spent little time in the northlands. Behind the priestess came four men carrying a large lacewood box by its brass handles. Although the box was closed and sealed, all who had gathered knew precisely what was inside.

The bearers placed the box onto the ground, settling the pale wooden box next to an opening in the soil. Not far away, a similar fresh patch of soil indicated where a burial had taken place the previous year. The ground was already cold enough that the diggers had been concerned, uncertain that they would be able to complete the excavation before the frost hit, but they had prevailed and been successful. As usual for a burial such as this one, none of the townspeople came to mourn and even the bearers, once the coffin had been delivered, made a hasty retreat. As they always did. As they had done for each similar burial. Nobody enjoyed spending any more time with the dead than absolutely necessary.

Particularly not these specific dead.

Once the hill was silent, the high priestess stepped forward and said a brief prayer, encouraging the soul of the deceased to move along to the hereafter in peace and beseeching the storm gods to assist in this endeavor, to guard and guide the spirit as it departed this life and entered the next. As though responding to her words, the flurry of snow increased, dancing through the gathered people and caressing each of them in turn.

Once the priestess finished her speech and the accompanying prayers, Malec stepped forward. Unlike the last such ceremony he had attended, he stood straight and tall, with no lingering sign of the Wasting that had so thoroughly ravaged his family. He placed a hand in silent tribute atop the casket, adding his own prayers to those uttered by the high priestess. Finally, he opened the lid, ever so slightly, just far enough to reach inside and place a carved wooden flute within. "This is yours," he said quietly. "Nobody else deserves to have this. Ever. Keep it with you and keep it safe."

Next to Malec, Leoni stood. Tears streamed down her face, enough for both her and the stoic man beside her. Northmen may have been capable of holding back their emotions and stopping the tears from forming until within the privacy of their own homes, but northwomen realized that there was no point in the delay. Emotions were meant to be shared and she owed the woman in the box everything. The least she could do was to show her the tears that she so profoundly deserved.

As the coffin slipped into its final resting place and the first spadefuls of frozen earth was cast in to cover it, Malec turned away. This would be the last such burial his family would ever need to endure; his sister had seen to that.

"This was exactly what she wanted," the tattooed woman stepped forward to offer her condolences as the group headed away. "She understood full well what was about to happen."

"Why didn't she save herself?" Malec turned his woeful gaze to the strange pair of women. "She knew she was about to die, so why didn't she take the cure when she found it?"

"She didn't want it." The answer, simple and direct, came from the cloaked woman. "Her only concern, the only thing that was ever on her mind, was finding the cure for you. So that you could marry your lady and have your family without the curse hanging over you."

"She's right," Leoni pointed out. "You would have been in that box had she not arrived when she did. We had already begun the preparations."

After being gone for more than a year, Malec's sister Keyt had returned only the week before. She had been almost dead upon arrival, having lost most of her body weight and coughing blood with every breath she took. She had ignored the pain, pushing through the exhaustion, as the Wasting continued to hemorrhage its way through her body. Not much had been left when she pressed the vial into Leoni's hands and collapsed on the ground next to her brother, never to stand again.

As Leoni, sobs of equal parts grief and relief, poured the water into Malec's unconscious mouth, Keyt's rattling, laborious breath had ceased forever.

Outside, the first snow of the season, unusually early, began to fall.

After life growing up in the beautifully rainy Pacific Northwest, Shanon L. Mayer tends to keep indoors, writing story after story, building vivid worlds on paper while her thoughts hold everything but images. She tends to look at everything in her world for inspiration – especially her collections of skulls, dragon statues, swords and knives, and pretty much anything that fits her eclectic, geeky-gothic lifestyle.

When her busy life feels like too much, she can be found relaxing with a hot mug of tea and a documentary on anything from theoretical physics to deep ocean wildlife to the most famous heists the world has ever seen.

The adventure continues in

Fallen Stars

Available in 2027

Keep reading for an exclusive sneak peek!

The familiar rocking motion eased Jasika into wakefulness. Thankfully she hadn't been summoned to defend against attackers the previous night, so she was much more refreshed than she had felt in quite some time. The air in her cabin was cool, leading her to realize that Keagan had already risen and left the cabin.

As her mind cleared from sleep, she slowly recognized that she was not on her bunk in her cabin. Instead, she was on a hard surface with neither pillow nor blanket. The familiar scent of the Temptress was nowhere to be found, replaced by unfamiliar odors and sounds. She cracked an eye, wondering where she was and how she had gotten there, and immediately regretted it. Perhaps this was still a dream, a nightmare from which she would awaken soon, a part of her hoped but the larger part of her knew better. She was on a strange ship, headed to gods-knew-where, and only the smallest of movements was required to confirm that she was chained to the wall.

Voices could be heard, most talking calmly in the distance and none that were recognizable. She remained still, not wanting to let her captors know that she had awoken, trying to sort out how she had gotten onto the boat and perhaps even to where she was being taken.

The first part was easy enough to resolve. She had been drugged, a needle laced with some noxious substance designed to render the target unconscious, had been used to knock her out in her own home. She knew the tactic well, as she had used the same trick on multiple occasions over the course of her life. Sometimes it was necessary when a target needed to be moved to a secondary location with as little struggle as possible and other times it was necessary to ensure that their killing was performed in complete silence. She took solace in the fact that she had been captured instead of killed outright. That would have been much more difficult to recover from.

The possibilities for the second part were endless. All four of the empires had a price of some weight on her head, as did many of the towns within the empires. Any of these bounties would be enough to warrant her capture, to risk the danger inherent in tracking someone as dangerous as she. Until they arrived, there was simply no way to know where she was being taken.

There were a handful of things that were in her benefit, she realized. Her eyepatch was still in place, as those who had captured her obviously didn't realize its value. She didn't have to move to recognize that the familiar weight of the daggers she always kept in the small of her back was missing, leaving her without weapons. *No surprise there*, she thought to herself. *I certainly wouldn't let a captive retain any of their weapons either.*

Slowly, she maneuvered her fingers across the shackles that tethered her to the wall. One of the first things she had been taught was the art of escaping all manner of restraints, but it was quickly apparent that these had been placed to thwart just such a skill. The shackles were placed just far enough apart that she couldn't quite reach them, even had she been able to find a suitable picking tool to use. *Why couldn't these men just be a little lazier?* That would have made escaping a much simpler task. *Perhaps I can twist my wrist around just a bit and reach the lock that way.*

She froze as one of the chains, jostled by her examination, rattled against the floor. While the sound wasn't loud, it was definitely noticeable if anyone was paying attention. She took a slow, deep breath, feigning sleep, and hoped that the rest of the boat's crew remained unaware.

"Hear that?" The voice dashed her hopes. "Sounds like she's waking up."

Sounds of scuffling echoed through the small room as the men, guards watching over her as she slept, pushed themselves to their feet. Jasika watched, warily, keeping her right eye closed and using only her left eye, hidden behind her magical eyepatch. Three men, one of whom she assumed had been the speaker she heard, came into view over the crates that formed a makeshift wall around her. All three looked dangerous, with cutlasses strapped to their hips. The sight gave Jasika hope as, once she freed herself from the shackles, all she would need to do was to take one of their swords and she would be back on even footing. Much as she disliked fighting with a cutlass, that didn't have any impact on her ability to do so. The biggest of them, a hulking man with wide shoulders, would be her first target.

While larger men were often stronger than their smaller counterparts, the cramped and confined space left him at a distinct disadvantage, particularly against Jasika's own small, agile form.

"Okay, then. Everybody out." The large man spared barely a glance over at their captive before heading across the chamber.

Jasika listened closely as they moved. From where they stood, they each took three strides across the floor, giving her an estimation of the size of the room in which she was trapped. A loud grating noise indicated the opening of a door and the telltale clicking sound of a key turning in the lock told her all she needed to know. Not only did she need to escape the shackles, but she needed to escape the room as well. The door sounded heavy and the lock sounded old, so her escape was bound to draw some attention.

It didn't matter. If she had to kill everyone on the boat in order to ensure her own safety, that would be what she would do. They had made a grave mistake in capturing her, of drawing her wrath. She had already been in a rotten mood before all of this had started and now they had given her a perfect outlet to express her displeasure. *Wouldn't be the first time,* she grumbled internally, *and probably won't be the last.*

Just as she was about to sit up and get a clearer view of her surroundings, a squeaking sound of hinges alerted her to additional movement. Now what? The sound was faint, nowhere near as loud as the door opening and closing had been, but it was immediately followed by a metallic click and the sound of glass shattering on the floor.

The scent reached her before the cloud did. Jasika recognized the sickly-sweet smell, as it belonged to a chemical she had used on multiple occasions, some recently. For that very reason, she kept a small capsule of antidote that would counter the effects of the gas in her clothing, tucked securely where she could reach it in an instant. She groped against her belt, but the shackles that continued to restrain her held her too securely. She couldn't reach the secret pocket, let alone the capsule contained within. *When I get back home,* she swore to herself, *I'm going to talk to Phemie. I need some of those protective sigils too.* It wasn't the first time she had considered getting tattoos that protected against various things, but she had hesitated, not wanting any identifiable

markings upon her body. Given the circumstances she currently found herself in, however,
she was beginning to rethink whether the benefit
outweighed the risk.

Jasika could hold her breath for almost five
minutes, nowhere near long enough for the gas
to clear and allow her to breathe freely once
more. Given what she could see of the space she
was in, and given how much of the smoky substance had already filled the space, the area would
be affected for many times that duration. Nevertheless, she sucked in a deep breath, intending to
hold out for as long as possible.

Masterful plan, she thought to herself as the
world around her darkened once more. *Just like
something I would do.*

* 9 7 8 1 9 5 8 0 7 6 2 7 9 *